I0575222

THE NOCTURNE CAGE TRILOGY **BOOK ONE**

POLYPHONIC SEDUCTION

Kit Englard

ARCANE LYRE

Content Guidance for the Nocturne Cage Series

This series contains mature themes, morally complex characters, and emotionally intense relationships.

At its heart, it is an exploration of consent, control, and the balance of power between supernatural beings—told through a lens of cultural depth, psychological nuance, and raw emotional stakes.

You can expect:

- Explicit sensuality, often entwined with magic and vulnerability
- Power exchange and restraint—always consensual, but not always soft
- Depictions of trauma and recovery, including flash-backs, panic, and moments of internal collapse
- Mental health themes: therapy, guilt, and inherited survival patterns
- Supernatural violence and emotional horror—intimate more than graphic
- Characters who make mistakes, lose control, and learn through fire

Nothing is included for shock value. Everything here is my attempt to explore the range of ethical dark fantasy. While this series isn't about safe love, it is about chosen love, and how love changes what's possible. If you seek stories of chaotic tenderness, power dynamics, and the slow, fierce work of healing through darkness—you belong here.

Please read at your own pace, and take care of your heart along the way.

– Kit

This is a work of fiction. Names, characters, organizations, and events are the
product of the author's imagination or used fictitiously. Any resemblance to
actual persons, living or dead, or real events is purely coincidental.

First edition
ISBN 979-8-9987117-0-1 (hardcover)
ISBN 979-8-9987117-1-8 (paperback)
ISBN 979-8-9987117-2-5 (ebook)

Cover and Interior design by Stewart Williams
Editing by Shawna Hampton

Published by Arcane Lyre Press, an imprint of Arcane Lyre LLC
Author website: https://kitenglard.com

Library of Congress Control Number: 2025906478

Library of Congress Subject Headings:
Fantasy fiction. 2. Paranormal romance. 3. Demons—Fiction. 4. Psychological
fiction. 5. Supernatural beings—Fiction.

BISAC Subject Headings:
FIC009050 FICTION / Fantasy / Dark Fantasy
FIC027120 FICTION / Romance / Paranormal / Demons
FIC025000 FICTION / Psychological

Author: Kit Englard
Title: Polyphonic Seduction / Kit Englard

Printed in the United States of America
10 9 8 7 6 5 4 3 2 1

Contents

Chapter One

Mia tilted her plastic cup, watching the last swirls of chai and melted ice drift at the bottom. The café hummed with voices and the soft strumming of indie music. Sound bounced off walls covered in bizarre pictures of goats. Sunlight slanted through the windows, making her squint as she tracked the steady flow of people coming and going. Her gaze dropped to the book bag at her feet, stuffed with final exams she'd come here to grade. She should open it. Get started. Instead, she slouched deeper into her chair, letting exhaustion settle into her bones. Students begging for extra credit or last-minute extensions drained her like never before, as if she were trying to reverse the flow of a glacier that had been moving for tens of thousands of years. It hadn't been this exhausting before. A week ago, she had felt like she was seeing the world through a veil. Now every interaction was sandpaper against an exposed nerve.

She brought the cup to her lips to try and get the last remnants of the spice blend she loved. Even after seventeen years of living in Canada, then the United States, the little girl who grew up on an uncharted island in the Arctic Ocean still marveled at the variety of flavors available in the world. That palate would probably expand when she traveled to Ecuador for the second time as part of her doctoral studies, where she would be studying glaciers on Andean volcanos at a remote field site.

A tingling energy tickled her skin, making her hair stand on end. The plastic cup crinkled in her tightening grip as she recognized the telltale sign of chaos magic. Her inner essence rumbled from behind the locked door in her mind, straining against its confines, answering the call before she could suppress it. She lifted her head sharply and scanned the café. Leaning against the counter stood a tall man with dark olive skin and piercing green eyes that shimmered even in the shadows. Pearlescent greens and vibrant indigo rippled like oil on water, as wisps of darkness danced and coiled. It was an echo of a sight she hadn't seen since exile. The hum of the café dulled, and she was wrenched back in time.

She stood on the tundra's edge, the wind a razor against her young face. Above, the aurora borealis churned, its colors bleeding across the night sky. It illuminated the snow in a dazzling show of colors. Her chest clenched—wonder, and fear, pressed on her ribs like ice under pressure. The lights had been the harbinger of her destruction, dooming her at birth to spend her long life wandering the human world as a ghost. Yet she couldn't help but be fascinated by their mystery.

"Miss, I brought you some coffee."

Mia jumped and stared at the barista, baffled. This wasn't the kind of place that *served* anything. The man leaned in close enough to brush against her shoulder. She recognized the deliberate move. *Stupid!* When she'd ordered, their hands had accidentally touched. Her amulet was gone, and that made her aura too strong. She jerked away and shook her head.

"You sure?" His brown eyes were entirely too interested.

This couldn't continue. If he didn't walk away now, he would keep pressing, keep asking, and sooner or later, he would notice that something about her wasn't human. The only way to stop him was to compel him, but controlling the range of her magic was nearly impossible. She took a slow, shaking breath, bracing against the invisible pressure building in her chest. If she used too much force, everyone in the café would obey. Too little, and he might resist and notice something was off. Her throat tightened. Whispering as softly as she could, she let the words slip past her lips like a blade unsheathing, sharp and precise. "Go away."

The barista's lips tipped into a frown.

For a moment Mia thought her spell hadn't worked. Then, slowly, he turned and went back behind the counter. Mia's heart pounded in her chest. Controlling him had been far easier than it should have been, but that's always how it went with humans. Another fun little *gift* left over from Divine Wars she was three thousand years too young to have experienced. Back then, it had been meant to corral panicking humans and keep them safe. Now, it just forced her people into hiding, and she was left to wander like a ghost among the living.

Her gaze caught on the man with the stunning aura. Her heart lurched. There was something there, lurking in the shadows that had dimmed the brightness of his eyes. A shiver ran down her back. It felt like he was breaking her down and analyzing every fractured piece. *I need to leave, he might have seen me do that.* Her hand was on her bag, zipping it shut. *Fucking disaster of a day...*

The bell above the door jingled, the sound slicing through the static-charged air. Mia's head snapped up as a petite brunette woman hesitated in the doorway, dark eyes darting like she was already searching for an exit. She clutched a worn paisley messenger bag to her hip, fingers digging into the fabric as if anchoring herself in place.

Mia's breath hitched. Her gaze flicked between the man and the woman. Both were lesser beings of chaos—sehru, born from the collision of human creativity and chaos magic. The brunette's eyes locked onto hers, and Mia exhaled, her tension easing slightly. Soft gold undertones flickered within the woman's petal-pink aura. No predatory essence clung to her, which meant she wasn't a threat. But the man at the counter was.

One shadowy predator of chaos. One light protector.

Mia knew so little about the wider world of chaos beings—born apart from them, sentenced to live among humans, unseen, unknown. She had spent years avoiding them. That was the rule. The only rule, really. Her essence leaned against its confines, drawn toward the scared sehru in front of her. When the Divine Wars ended and the king of gods sealed the Heavenly Gates, those left behind fractured into groups. Over millennia, their descendants hunted each other, sometimes to extinction. It was why her people had been driven from Uruk, the cradle of their existence. The lamassu, the most powerful of the protective nishutu soldiers, had been created to guard the righteous, and to shield humanity from war. But that instinct and purpose had made the lamassu vulnerable to those who craved power. It was a weakness their enemies had exploited until her kind were little more than whispers in forgotten texts.

Whatever was happening here wasn't good. Interfering was dangerous. *Leave, moron,* she ordered herself. Her fingers wrapped around the strap of her bag, but her feet refused to move.

One cautious step at a time, the woman walked closer. Her movements jerky, as if she was fighting against an unseen current. She reached into the pocket of her bag and extracted her phone. Rapidly, she typed out a message and held up the screen. Hello, I'm Piper.

Mia sat frozen in place. She had a split second to decide if she was going to talk to this woman. Blood rushed in her ears. The ache inside her, the one she had buried for years, let out a mournful, rumbling cry. This was a chance to talk to someone like herself. The woman wasn't the shadowy man in the corner. Creatures of light wouldn't hunt each other, right?

Piper's frown deepened, then she turned to walk away.

Mia clumsily got out of her chair and tapped the

woman's shoulder. She fished out her phone and typed out a reply message. Mia.

The woman's thin pink lips curved into the shadow of a smile. She tucked the phone back into a pocket, then set the bag at her feet. Her hands free, she pointed at Mia, then collapsed her hands into parallel fists twice. Her brows raised slightly in a question. "Do you know sign?"

"Yes," Mia signed back slowly. It seemed impossible that she ran into not only another chaos being, but one who inexplicably knew American Sign Language. "Are you Deaf?"

Piper bent her wrist, making her fist nod in the sign for yes. "You?"

"No…"

"I'm a muse. What are you?"

She hesitated. Telling anyone about her true nature would put her people at risk. Her one reason for being was to keep them safe. She dredged up the lie her adoptive father had suggested she tell. Something that would explain why she couldn't talk, without giving away what she was. "I'm a Siren. Our voices aren't safe for humans."

Mia's thoughts stalled as she immediately realized her mistake. That lie worked fine when her essence wasn't about to spill out onto the floor. Sirens were sehru and wouldn't have near the level of magic she did.

Piper's eyes narrowed. For a split second, Mia thought she was going to call her bluff. Then the muse relaxed. "Oh, I see. Good thing I'm Deaf, then." She smiled shyly. "I know it's silly. What's the point of a muse who's Deaf, right?"

"I thought you did more than just music?"

"We do, but my husband is a musician. A violinist." Piper's hands shook with nerves. "Doesn't matter. Do you know where I can get a bus out of the city?"

Mia frowned, taken aback by the question and growing more suspicious that there was something off about this woman. "There's a Greyhound station. If you take a 61 bus, you'll get downtown. You'll just have to walk a little."

"How much does it cost?"

"I don't remember. I have a bus pass loaded on my student ID."

"I need help—" Piper's hands trembled. She swallowed hard, glancing at the exit. "I—"

"There you are!" A familiar woman's voice floated over the noise.

Mia missed the rest of Piper's signs as Sage, a woman who lived a few floors down from her, came over. Her short, curly brown hair bounced as she walked.

Piper's face drained of what little color it had.

Sage's arm draped around Piper's shoulders, her fingers digging in a little too hard. Her smile was bright, easy. "Thanks for keeping her company. She gets anxious sometimes, don't you, Piper?"

Mia's gaze flicked between them. Piper was rigid, her body coiled tight like a rabbit caught in a snare. Every muscle braced for the moment she'd have to decide if she could run at all. Mia signed, "Is she your friend?"

Piper pinched her lips together and gave an almost imperceptible shake of her head.

"She's been a little paranoid since she got out of the

hospital," Sage continued. "Hallucinations, memory lapses...doctor says it's temporary."

An earthy, gritty taste spread on Mia's tongue as her magic sensed the lie.

Sage dragged Piper toward the entrance. "I just came to pick her up. I'll make sure she gets home safely."

Piper threw a frantic glance back at Mia in wild-eyed panic as she was pulled out of the café. Mia stared after them in stunned silence. Her gaze drifted down to Piper's bag. She grabbed it as she raced after the two women, catching up to them just before they turned up the block back toward their apartment building.

"You left this," Mia signed, then held up the bag. Sage went to grab it, but Mia pulled it out of the way and strode to Piper. She could sense the woman's fear radiating from her. Something deep inside Mia stirred, stretching awake. A low growl vibrated through her bones. Just give her the bag and leave, she thought forcefully. Pressure built up in her chest, until she thought she would suffocate. An overwhelming need to protect washed over her. She leaned forward as she pressed the bag into Piper's hands, and inhaled. A wisp of Piper's life force tangled with her own, taking root in her soul. With her exhale, she let a sliver of herself slip free, sinking into the muse.

"Look at that. You made a friend." Sage's sharp gaze flicked to Mia's hand still resting on Piper's. "But Piper's got enough of those, don't you?" Sage pushed Mia back and took Piper by the shoulders, steering her away. "You won't have to worry about her anymore."

Mia watched helplessly as her new charge was dragged away, every instinct screaming at her to intervene. Without more information, that was impossible. Her magic already pulled her into something dangerous, she didn't have to dig her own grave by letting that instinct run wild. *I'll find you,* she promised silently. When a lamassu marked someone for protection, it was a sacred vow that wasn't easily broken. Already she could feel Piper's petal-soft essence nesting inside her golden fire. Mia's heart fluttered in a mix of exhilaration and dread. This wasn't supposed to happen. The amulet had always kept her divine essence locked away, suppressing the pull of her magic, keeping her invisible. Without it, that control was unraveling. If she could feel that shift, then so could other chaos beings.

She pivoted and walked back into the café. It was a small relief when she found that her things were still where she'd left them, and she slid back into her chair. Getting involved in whatever Piper was mixed up in was a good way to end up dead. She had no way of knowing if the woman was associated with any chaos hunters or other danger. Her foot tapped restlessly under the table. Before the Divine Wars, lamassu had been protectors. Now, they sat on their island, eking out an existence while they prayed for Enlil and Ninlil to open the Heavenly Gates and let them join their brethren.

Fat chance of that happening, she thought grimly. Once, she'd believed they would take pity on her. That they would return, undo her exile, and save her from being tossed into a world she was never meant to navigate alone. But they never came. Her fingers worked at the strap of her book bag. Piper's fear and desperation wormed their way into her mind, stirring something that lurked deep inside. She'd been scared like that once.

The memory swallowed her whole.

She stood on the deck of a boat, watching as the Arctic Ocean swallowed the shore of her home. The sun shone overhead during the time of perpetual light, warming her face, while the smell of brine and frost filled her lungs. A sharp summer wind whipped her face, chasing away the warmth of the sun. It stimulated the darkness inside her, nurturing it until shadowed tendrils wormed into her soul. She'd known that she was destined to die, known she'd been chosen as this century's maru hiptu sacrifice. It was a solemn duty, she was told. An honor to be able to protect the last of her people by living among the humans so that the rest of her kind could live in blissful ignorance of the outside world. She clutched the heavy amulet the matriarch had secured around her neck, as if she could lessen the weight of the burden. The only companion on her journey would be a stranger.

Gordon, the maru hiptu sacrifice from a century before, took a drag of his cigarette and blew out a cloud of smoke. While he'd been raised by his predecessor like he was supposed to be, Gordon had abandoned her the second he'd dropped her off at a boarding school in the middle of the Great Bear Rainforest in British Columbia. The only times in her life he showed up was to sign paperwork.

You're not dead, Mia reminded herself, dragging her thoughts back to the present. The funeral, the eulogies, the death shroud, the ashes. It had all been a carefully or-chestrated performance designed to keep the troubles of the world from stirring the protective instincts of the la-massu and luring them to their own destruction. Even her parents were shielded from temptation, since you couldn't defend a dead girl.

Golden magic flared. She snatched up her bag. She was done being a ghost. Done being invisible. A fluttering of ex-citement in her stomach forced its way through the dark-ness that had grown and festered over the last seventeen years. She seized that sensation, tucking it away. Help-ing Piper was a lot better than grading hundreds of engi-neering exams from apathetic students. Exciting, even. A chance to prove, once and for all, that she was *alive*.

Chapter Two

sidore inhaled deeply as the mysterious, dark auburn-haired chaos woman hastily gathered her things. Even through the overpowering aroma of roasting coffee beans, he caught a hint of frost and salt water. She wasn't like him, a sehru. His ancestors were lesser creatures shaped by human imagination tangling with chaos magic.

She was a nishutu.

His pulse quickened. Her ancestors had been forged by Enlil, king of the gods, to wage war against the divine rebels who challenged his rule. The only ones he ever crossed paths with were members of the Storm Feathers, a rival cabal operating in the Northeast—and they barely considered his kind worthy of shining their shoes. They were also demonic, not protective.

A tingling sensation ran down his spine, and energy flooded his limbs. *What is she doing here?* he wondered. More than anything, he wanted to chase after her, to understand what she was.

That soft ripple of compulsion magic she'd used had been so subtle, he almost missed it. His own magic could tease, lure, seduce, but he could never force. And the sweet little protective nishutu had *hated* it. He saw it in the way her hands had gripped the edge of the table. She hadn't taken any pleasure in it, although he thought it would be justified. The way that barista had been leering had his demon coiling in agitation. Humans were nothing compared to a nishutu. That man didn't deserve to kiss the ground she walked on, much less think he could stake his claim on her.

His thoughts drifted. Her face had an elegant, predatory beauty—high cheekbones, a slender nose that curved into the barest hook, and heart-shaped lips painted in dusty mauve that complimented her dark sandstone skin. On her wrist there was a tattoo with markings he'd never seen. The ink was arranged in a series of lines and wedge-like symbols, and it hummed with old magic. The ancient stuff that only truly old nishutu species could wield. But it was her scent that intrigued him most. There was something achingly familiar about it, laced with magic he could almost taste but couldn't name. It was delectable. He forced himself to take a slow sip of his coffee, waiting for time to slip past so he could follow without being noticed. The aura surrounding her had been a mix of pale earth-toned reds and oranges. It all but confirmed that she was a protective spirit. There had been a handful of them created during the Divine Wars to shield humanity from annihilation. The surviving gods had searched tirelessly for their precious guardians, not wanting to leave them behind to be devoured by the nightmares that roamed the earthly realm. And yet here she was. Sitting in a café, in plain sight.

Frustration gnawed at his insides like tiny termites. His fangs ached, reminding him that it had been too long since he'd eaten more than the blood he'd gotten from his dealer. *You're only interested in her because you're hungry,* he chastised himself. The empty cardboard cup collapsed in his viselike grip. That wasn't the only reason he was interested in her, and he knew it. If she wasn't claimed, she was a walking target. Maybe she didn't realize how much danger she was in. Maybe she did, and she thought she could handle it.

Time's up, he thought as his mouth curved into a smile. He chucked his mangled coffee cup into a waste bin and left the café. It was a warm May afternoon. The sidewalks were full of people enjoying the break from the spring rains, and he kept having to turn sideways to avoid directly touching anyone. Even with a long-sleeved shirt on, the cold skin of a lamia demon would be off-putting even if a human didn't know what he was. He opened his mouth and caught the faintest hint of frost on his tongue. His smile broadened and he stuffed his hands into the pockets of his jeans as he walked down the hill. The scent had him turning right at the next intersection. He passed house after house, most built in the mid-twentieth century with classic brick. The architecture of Pittsburgh fascinated him. In some ways it reminded him of his home in Philadelphia. Not that it was a good idea to share that opinion with the locals. When he'd arrived here, he'd discovered that the smaller city had something of an inferiority complex that it liked to take out on its more populous counterpart on the eastern side of the state. Personally, he blamed the steel mill collapse in the '70s for that problem. Still, he loved the city with its mix of old Victorian homes, modern high-rises, and everything in between. Like the houses didn't have to choose if they were going to be fancy or full of holes—they all belonged just the same.

Isidore halted outside of an old apartment building. He took in the structure. It had white and terra-cotta brick that accented the designer's attempt at mimicking a gothic-style architecture. A vibrant green lawn stretched out in front of the building, and a set of concrete stairs cut through a small hill that led to the front door. No shadows deep enough to hide in. No signs of a deadly chaos hunter lurking inside. But that didn't mean the nishutu was safe.

His earlier excitement of finding her faded. There was no way it was a coincidence that the hunters lived in the same building as a rare protective nishutu. He raked his fingers through his hair and turned to walk back up the street. She should have been marked. A sigil, a token. Something that told the world she was claimed. Without it, she was either unaffiliated, reckless, or running from something. *Arrogant idiot,* he thought irritably. He should just leave her to deal with the consequences. If the Storm Feathers got to her first, that was on her. A quiet hiss escaped his lips. The rival cabal had secured their dominance by systematically hunting down and eliminating powerful nishutu factions for centuries. *Sadistic bastards,* he cursed. The idea of one of those feathered fuckers getting their talons in a protective nishutu made his skin crawl. It went against what little moral fiber he'd developed.

He turned onto the busy commercial road. A pair of teenagers laughed at an inside joke as they waited for a bus. A woman with a stroller was enjoying an Italian ice. The muscles in his arms tensed as his mood darkened. His father wasn't going to be thrilled with his report. There was too much about the hunters he still didn't know.

His car was tucked into a shady spot in one of the paid lots. He walked up to the door and touched the handle. The headlights flickered, illuminating the bushes that practically brushed up against the low black hood of the Mercedes S-Class AMG. The leather seat squeaked as he sank into it. He set his phone in the dashboard stand, opened up the app they used to make encrypted calls, and clicked on his father's name. An overly cheerful jingle played three times before his father's face filled the screen.

"One thing I'll say about you, is that you're always on time," his father said with a smile that didn't *quite* reach his electric green eyes. "Did you find the hunter?"

Isidore swallowed a sigh as he prepared to face the inevitable disappointment. "I've narrowed it down to one of two people. A man named Jayce Robertson and a woman who goes by Sage Halloway. Jayce is a real name—I was able to find records going back to high school. He was a mediocre student who suddenly manifested a talent on the violin his sophomore year. He went to the Curtis Institute of Music in Philadelphia."

His father's thick, unruly brows knit together. "Is he connected to any of the hunter clans?"

"I don't think so. He's married to a woman named Piper Nelson, but I only saw her for the first time today..." His stomach clenched, and he swallowed. "I think they've got her trapped in that apartment. She's a sehru, I'm certain of that. I think she might be a muse. They got married young. She was a student at the Art Institute of Philadelphia while he was at Curtis, although she didn't graduate. I don't have a clear read on what clan she's affiliated with, if any."

"Mm...That would explain the miraculous talent. What else have you learned?"

Here we go. Isidore took a fortifying breath. "I found practically everything on Jayce. Every one of his leases up until now only includes his and Piper's names. Sage doesn't have a paper trail. I'm guessing she's the hunter, but I don't understand how Jayce fits in with this."

His father grunted. "Dimitra *insisted* you were ready for this. I thought you'd have enough for me to confirm that the hunter was from the Venator Mons clan! We cannot send an elimination team out there unless we're certain where she's from. It's too much of a risk to accidentally start a war with a hunter clan we know nothing about. It could compromise our position with our tributaries if hunters start showing up and snatching people off the streets."

It was always politics with his father and sister. His stomach twisted and churned. For months he'd been training under Dimitra, learning the ropes of working intelligence ever since he lost his appetite for the more violent jobs. "I know! Except for this Jayce guy, the hunter seems to be working alone."

"A lone hunter means that they've got an agenda, and we need to know what it is. The leader of Venator Mons wasn't forthcoming."

Isidore's grip on the steering wheel tightened until his knuckles turned white. "There's something else. Another woman lives in the building—a nishutu. I only just found out today. It's possible the hunter has her marked as the next target."

His father's eyes narrowed to slits. "What kind of nishutu?"

"A protective one, I don't know what species."

"What group do they have allegiance with?"

Isidore's heart thudded. "I don't know."

"What do you know?"

"She's powerful."

"Isidore…" His father let out a frustrated, rattling, hiss. "We can't get tangled up in something we don't under-stand. I want you to just wait and watch."

"Let me warn her at least, so she can get out." He hated the plea in his tone. Something in his gut told him that woman was in way over her head. "She was walking around without any kind of allegiance mark. I think—"

"If she belongs to no one, she's up for grabs," his father snapped. "If she's hiding, someone will come looking. And if she's on the run, we'd be inviting her enemies to our doorstep. Stay in your lane, and let her and her allies deal with whatever comes. We can't risk starting a feud with forces we can't even identify. If you recklessly pick a fight with the wrong one, then we'll just attract fire."

His breathing turned shallow. He saw another nishutu, a man, dead at his feet. Not just a protective nishutu, but a divine one. Crafted from the primordial waters of Nammu, and tasked with condemning the wicked and protecting the righteous. The sukkalu had offered himself—his blood, his life—just to keep Isidore alive. Divinity traded for corruption, only for Isidore to have lied and reported the nishutu was a lowly sehru. And for what? For him to turn his back the first time someone needed him?

"Isidore."

He jerked his head up.

His father's expression softened. "You can't take responsibility for every lost chaos being, just because of one mishap. That sehru was a protective entity, duty bound to defend others. He gave his life for yours, as our natures intended."

"But—"

"Enough! It's been eight months. The brooding needs to end. Find a way to get your head on straight before you come home. I want an update in a week."

The phone beeped as the call ended. Isidore stayed stock still as his arms trembled. His shoulders heaved with each angry breath. A tremor ran up his arms. His ribs constricted like a vise. "Shit!" He slammed his palms against the steering wheel, the impact sending a shock up his arms. At this rate he was going to have the bodies of two women laid out at his feet. Oh, sure. He wouldn't be the one standing over the corpses with a bloodstained knife. But when he died and inevitably landed in front of Geshtinanna, who would document the record of his life, he'd still have to add two more innocent souls who died because he didn't want to upset Daddy.

He raked his fingers through his hair as he tried to pull his thoughts together. If she was unaffiliated, stepping in could be seen as a claim to whomever was after her. The House of Crimson Fang didn't interfere with outsiders unless they were worth the cost of protection. If she had enemies, they would become his enemies. If she had debts, they would be his to collect. He would be placing her under his name, his house, his protection. But the idea of two more entries on his already crowded ledger was too much. Especially the nishutu. His father had never been locked in a cage, starving, waiting for someone to decide if he lived or died. "I'll just sneak into her apartment, warn her, and help her escape. Then I can go back to figuring this out." He blew out a puff of air as the tightness in his chest eased. Quick. Clean. His father would never know, and he wouldn't have another dead nishutu etched into his conscience.

Chapter Three

Papers sprawled out on the table as Mia tried to finish her grading. Her encounter with Piper made focusing on anything impossible, but saying she was going to intervene on Piper's behalf and finding a way to do that without compromising herself in the process had become a roadblock. She took a sip of her Amarone wine, letting the rich notes of sandalwood and plum linger on her tongue. It was an indulgence and overdramatic to pair it with an activity like grading. But the wine was just one of the little reminders in her life that proved she was alive.

She smiled to herself as she set the glass down. Gordon would probably be proud of her, if the man were capable of feeling anything toward her at all. His survival strategy seemed to hinge on drowning himself in alcohol, drugs, and sex. For a long time she'd hated her adoptive father for abandoning her. Now? She wondered if she'd dodged a bullet. If she had to choose between isolation and being forced to spend her time with a man who didn't care about anything but himself? The isolation was better. At least you knew where you stood.

A sharp tug at her chest left her breathless. Piper's constant anxiety was like having a needle poking at her all day. Not enough to break skin, but unpleasant all the same when her charge's nerves spiked. Restless energy overcame her. Sitting here doing nothing was useless. Piper needed her to be working out how to save her, not mindlessly grading. She stood and stalked to the entryway, grabbing her purse and keys, then strode out the door. After locking it, she slid her keys into the pocket of her jeans before heading toward the stairs.

Only the faint tether linking her to Piper led her toward the apartment the muse was living in. Sage had only moved into the building after Mia's roommate had moved out. Her stomach clenched as her mind wandered to her missing amulet. It wasn't just a trinket, it had been given to her by the matriarch on the day of her ritual drowning. She had stood there, shivering as icy water slid down her skin, while the leader of her people fastened the amulet around her throat like a collar, binding her to a fate she hadn't chosen. Chains of violet magic had encircled her divine essence, weighed it down like an anchor dragging a victim to their watery death. Mia shuddered and pushed the memory away. *I should have just lived alone,* she thought irritably. Her chest ached just at the thought. Roommates had drawbacks, but the idea of living alone sent a chill through her. That would be true isolation. Plus, the amulet being gone was almost a relief. The thing might have protected her, but it also had left her feeling like a shell of a person. Since it went missing, things felt sharper. Colors were more vibrant. Sound more rich.

She halted at an unadorned apartment door. It looked identical to all the others, but Mia knew that something was going on inside. Her heart felt like it would beat out of her chest. She only ever interacted with humans when she needed to for work or school. Taking a breath, she rapped on the door and dug her phone out of her purse as she waited.

The seconds stretched. Then a sharp click, and the door swung open. Sage stood there, brows drawn together. "Hey, what are you doing here?"

It dawned on her then that she probably should have come up with a plan. *Great job.* She quickly typed on her phone. I was just grading and thought I'd come by and see how Piper is doing.

"She's fine, just resting," Sage replied smoothly. Then her lips tipped up in a slow smile. "Actually, this is perfect timing. We were just about to head out for drinks. You should come."

That all-too-familiar earthen taste of a lie was back. They hadn't intended on going out moments ago. A tiny part of her knew that it was her sudden appearance that had caused the change. *Don't be paranoid, Mia. Humans are always asking you to spend time with them.* She studied Sage's expression. There was no hint that she was under Mia's influence. Dread spread like a poison. At the café, Sage hadn't responded to her either. *She's using something to block me.* Which meant Sage knew about magic.

Mia swallowed and brushed away the nerves. Even if they knew about magic, it didn't mean they knew about her. There were very few things that would truly block any lamassu's magic. Those things weren't cheap, or easy to come by. Mia's chest tightened. This was exactly the kind of outing she wanted, a way to learn more about them before she did something stupid. Even if the thing was protecting Sage from her alluring aura, it would be nothing in the face of the full strength of her divine magic. *You can do this*, she thought as she typed. Yeah, that'd be great.

"Just one second." Sage stepped inside.

Mia shifted her weight from one foot to the next as she waited for them to return. The anticipation was agonizing. *This is a terrible idea*, she thought. Inserting herself into a potential domestic abuse situation was just not the smart and safe thing to do. But did she want safe? That was how she'd always run her life. Work hard. Get stellar grades. Get into the school program. Study science, it was the next big thing. Except her heart had drawn her to environmental engineering because she'd read a bit too much *National Geographic* and decided she was going to save the planet. Her stomach twisted into knots. *You can't just leave her.* She let out a slow, deliberate breath. The decision to involve herself was already made. Piper was her charge. Her responsibility.

She jumped as the door opened and Sage and a man appeared. He had dirty-blond hair flopped into his acne-splotched pale face. The corner of his lips were tipped downward, as if he were perpetually trapped in a state of deep concentration.

"This is Jayce," Sage said as she locked her door and jerked her head in the direction of the blond man.

They all headed out into the cool evening air. It usually relaxed her to go for walks after dark, but both Sage and Jayce were moving stiffly at her side. Not wanting to waste a moment of her chance to get some real information out of Sage, she activated the text-to-speech on her communication app so it would read aloud what she typed. "Are you two dating?"

"Ah…" Jayce started awkwardly. "No, we're roommates."

Sage jumped in. "I met Jayce when we were living in Philadelphia. He was studying at the Curtis Institute of Music—do you know it?"

Mia shook her head.

"It's one of the best music schools in the world. Jayce is a solo violinist now."

"Is that what you're doing in Pittsburgh?" Mia typed as a monotoned female voice read her words. Her mind was turning. Piper had said she was married to a violinist.

Jayce straightened, puffing out his chest like he was on stage. "Yeah! I've got some symphony concerts lined up—real music, you know? Not like that overproduced stuff you listen to." His eyes flicked to her T-shirt.

Mia's thumb twitched in annoyance as it hovered over the touch screen. She recognized forced arrogance when she saw it. Florence and the Machine wasn't exactly mainstream pop anymore. "I listen to all kinds of stuff."

Sage shot a glare at Jayce. The conversation died down

and they finished their walk in silence. When Jayce opened the iconic red door to The Cage, a wave of smoke smacked into Mia's senses. She followed her companions inside and found a table as Sage got them a round of beers and put in their food order. Mia let her gaze drift around the room. It was just as packed for a Friday night as she expected. The crowd was a mix of businessmen, students, and anyone in between. It was almost enough to have her shrug off her problems and embrace the atmosphere. Except that Jayce was staring at her with an intensity that sent a shiver up her spine.

She pulled out the Bluetooth keyboard and set the phone on a stand so that it was easy for him to see the text. The computer voice still spoke, but it was barely audible over the din. "Bad week?"

He gave his shoulders a shake. "Just a little intense. Some stuff got in the way of my practicing."

Mia nodded vaguely. "Do you know a woman named Piper? I met her at a café yesterday."

His already thin lips disappeared as he pressed them together.

Sage appeared holding their beers, set them down, and slid Mia's across the table. "What are we talking about?"

"She asked about Piper," Jayce said stiffly.

"Oh, don't worry about her. She's a friend of mine who's staying with us. Been going through a lot of medical stuff and needed someone to look out for her." Sage sat down and took a drink from her beer. "Sorry if she said anything weird."

Mia tapped her burnt-sienna painted nails on the beer glass. She didn't need her magical lie-detecting abilities to tell that Sage was lying through her teeth. It wasn't impossible for a chaos being to have mental health challenges, but it seemed unlikely that one would willingly submit to being inpatient at a hospital. "I'm sorry to hear that. She seemed nice, and I haven't seen her at any of the Deaf events in town."

"You wouldn't, she's not from here," Sage replied smoothly. "She mostly works as a freelance digital artist."

That at least made sense. A Deaf muse seemed like they would naturally gravitate toward something like visual arts. Mia grabbed her beer and took a long drink. The familiar malty taste from a local brewery helped her to focus. Piper had said her husband was a violinist. Jayce fit the description, but something about the way he acted unsettled her.

"Where're you from?" Jayce asked sharply.

Mia swallowed and put her fingers back to the keys. "Canada."

Sage laughed. "Seriously?"

"Yeah. I'm from Baffin Island," she lied, without remorse. If these two were comfortable with keeping secrets, so was she.

Jayce smirked. "Do you play hockey?"

She didn't miss the condescending tone. Her fingers drummed on her keyboard as she considered her reply. "No, soccer. I wasn't very good."

Sage laughed with a delicate, bell-like tone that didn't

match her undertow of malice. "We should hang out more. You're my kind of person. Jayce was just telling me about his fantasy hockey team…"

Mia let her mind drift, but a nagging tension settled in her chest. They still hadn't mentioned Piper. She tried to focus enough to pick up on some information they dropped. Jayce was twenty-four. Sage wasn't from Philadelphia originally, but moved there when she'd finished school. It turned out she was twenty-seven. And still, neither of them mentioned Piper. She tried bringing her up, but each time they brought the conversation back around to something about Jayce's career.

Her vision blurred. She blinked hard, trying to clear it, but the edges of the room softened, like watercolors bleeding together. "Sage, what fo tou do for wrk?" She frowned down at her fingers. It felt like she was moving through a vat of maple syrup.

Sage let out one of her gratingly high, fake laughs, the kind meant to shift the focus. "I'm a photographer. Always moving around." The chair scraped against the floor as she stood. "I think you've had enough to drink."

Mia went to type on the keyboard, but it felt like the keys kept slipping out from under her fingertips. A garbled string of nonsense came out in the same monotoned woman's voice.

Sage laughed, then stood behind her and helped her up. "I didn't peg you for a lightweight."

That didn't feel right—it took a lot more alcohol than this to get her drunk. Mia's legs buckled as she tried to push away from Sage. Jayce lunged around the table and caught her. Heat prickled her skin, and sweat beaded, then rolled down her back.

All it would take was a few words laced with magic to compel them to let her go. She just had to focus. Weak sparks of magic came to her call and she imbued her words with it. "Put…me…down."

Jayce's hold loosened as her feeble spell took hold. She jerked free, only to stumble and crash to the floor. He grunted in irritation and bent down to haul her back up.

"I've got her purse and stuff." Sage dropped the false niceties. "Let's go."

Mia gathered up her magic to add more weight to her spell, but Sage covered her mouth with a hand before she could get the words out. Colors and sound bled together. *Stupid idiot,* Mia thought viciously as her heart rate slowed. The world faded to gray at the edges, then she tumbled into darkness.

~

Cold dampness pressed against her skin as Mia's awareness trickled back. The scent of earth and grass filled her nose, and plastic zip ties dug into her skin at her wrists and ankles. She struggled against the bindings, but they held firm. A rolled-up bit of cloth that was stuffed into her mouth muffled her gasping breaths. It was damp with saliva and tied in place so tightly that the corners of her lips burned. Her mind fought through the rising panic as she tried to make sense of what was happening. She lay at the base of a steep hill, shadowy trees looming overhead.

"Finally," someone said from behind her.

She recognized Jayce's tenor voice and froze.

"No more dead weight. No more being shackled to a second-rate muse. Once we drain her, I'm going to bury that bitch."

"Don't get ahead of yourself," Sage muttered.

Terror surged through Mia's veins. Piper. He was talking about Piper, was going to kill her. Rage and panic drew out a deep, throaty growl from her chest. She yanked at her restraints, wrists burning against the plastic ties. *Get out, get out, get out!* her mind screamed as she struggled against her bindings.

Jayce's attention snapped to Mia. "Sage!"

Panic crashed over her, drowning out everything else. The magic inside her roared to the surface. Electric, opalescent power seized control and flooded her veins. Her bones shifted and cracked. Skin split. A roar ripped from her throat, ricocheting off the trees, and the leaves shivered in its wake. Her T-shirt shredded as a pair of earth-red, feathered wings unfolded from her back. Inhuman strength rushed in. The zip ties holding her wrists and ankles snapped. Mia scrambled to her feet and lurched into a run, her wings beating frantically as she tried to get airborne.

Chaos magic swelled behind her. "No, you don't get to just leave!" Sage raged as she thrust out a hand, power crackling in her fingertips. The spell hurtled toward Mia.

"I will rip those wings off myself if I have to!"

The bolt of magic grazed the tip of Mia's wing, and she let out a screech of pain. She willed her muscles to work harder, faster. Her wings stretched wide and caught a current of air. Then, at last, her feet left the ground. Sweat drenched her back as she gasped for air. She reached the leafy canopy and streaked forward, branches lashing against her bare skin. Her shoulder muscles ached and her wings slowed. She was losing altitude, then plummeting toward the ground. She screamed. Her body skidded against rocks that carved up her skin, and she came to an abrupt halt as she splashed into a stream.

Twigs snapped as Sage and Jayce forced their way through a thicket. Mia stumbled to her feet, only to slam into a solid chest. Cold fingers wrapped around her waist. Her claws extended and sliced into flesh. It took her mind a moment to process that it was a man in front of her, one who looked vaguely familiar. His eyes glimmered an eerie emerald green. He opened his mouth and a snakelike forked tongue brushed her cheek, fluttering like the wings of a moth as her heart hammered against her ribs.

The man's head jerked up at the sound of people trying to push through shrubs. "Time to go." He hoisted her over his shoulder like she was nothing as he took off running. Shrubs whipped past, lashing her skin. Mia was too petrified to fight. Her surroundings spun, and she closed her eyes, pressing her forehead to the stranger's back. The rhythm of his movements was impossibly smooth, as if he wasn't running through tangled roots and uneven ground at all. A cold, shadowy magic closed in, blanketing them in silence.

After what felt like hours, they came to a stop. Her rescuer set her down on a flat gray stone. Unnatural darkness sealed them inside a tight ring of eerie light. She caught her breath as her eyes fixed on the stranger. Forest green scales, outlined in onyx, shimmered as he moved. His hair was a thick, wavy black that shifted like smoke.

He caught his breath, chest heaving. "You okay?"

Her body trembled as her gaze flicked nervously across his face, taking in every predatory detail. She had nothing to use to communicate—no phone, no whiteboard. She took a shaking breath. *He's not human, you won't mesmerize him by just talking.* It had been so long since she'd used her voice to talk to anyone, since she'd properly spoken. She licked her lips. "Yeah. Who are you?" The words felt awkward, and she could hear the thick accent she'd never been able to get rid of.

He shifted from one foot to the other, his movements as smooth as a serpent as he studied her. "Isidore. You?"

"Mia."

"You can't go back to your apartment."

She gaped. "Of course I'm—" Her breath hitched. "Where else would I go?"

"Your apartment is in the same building as those hunters. You can't go back. Do you have somewhere else to stay?"

Her chest tightened and she got unsteadily to her feet. This man could be just as dangerous as the hunters. Her muscles tensed, preparing to bolt. "How do you—" She exhaled sharply as the words tangled up. "How the hell do you know where I live?"

Isidore dragged a hand down his face. "I was looking for those hunters when I saw you at the café yesterday."

Recognition slammed into her. "You—you were at the café!"

His gaze was fixed determinedly on her face. "Yeah. Look, do you have somewhere safe to stay or not?"

Thoughts flitted through her mind in disordered bursts. "I can…find a hotel?" Her voice was thin, almost feeble to her ears. "Shit! My purse is still with them!" A wave of dizziness came over her, and she fell back onto the stone slab. Her heart rate evened out as she took long breaths. The chill against her skin made her shiver. First her shoulders, then down her arms, her stomach. Slowly, her mind started to work through everything. Her breath hitched. The air shouldn't feel like this. Her heart rate skyrocketed and she snapped her arms across her chest and twisted her shoulders, blocking his view. *Oh gods, I'm naked. In a park. With a strange man.* Shoes scraped the earth, and she drew her knees up.

"Here."

She glanced over her shoulder. Isidore stood holding out his button-down shirt. His scaled chest drew her attention, and she jerked her eyes up toward his face.

"Take it."

Hesitantly, she reached out one hand while keeping the other clamped around her chest. She turned her back to him. Her wings needed to be pulled back in. Panic ripped a pathetic, clipped, high-pitched whine from her throat.

"What's wrong?"

Her face burned with shame. Now she was naked *and* incompetent. "I don't remember how to change back."

There was silence broken only by the scuffing of shoes against dirt. "Suck the magic back into your bones."

"My bones?" she asked in the same rasping whine.

"Where do you imagine your magic goes normally?"

"A closet."

There was a quiet, whistling hiss. When Isidore spoke, his voice was thin with frustration. "Imagine putting it back in the closet."

She focused on slowing her breaths, and her heart naturally followed suit. Closing her eyes, she felt for the magic that sparked and crackled along her skin. She imagined seizing hold of it, and stuffing it back into the bottom of a closet like cloth. It surged and broke free.

"Tiamat's tits…" he muttered. "No control. You don't have a safe house…Bleeding kur." He rolled his shoulders, stretching the tension from his muscles. "Just put the shirt on backward."

Tears pricked at her eyes and she put the shirt on like a smock. She couldn't bear to face him. Her hands shook as she wrapped her arms around herself to keep the garment in place.

Isidore walked slowly around her, keeping a respectable distance. If he was embarrassed, there was no hint of it. "Do you have any friends you can stay with?"

She shook her head, watching every move he made.

His lip pulled back, revealing sharp fangs.

"What are you?" she blurted out before she could stop herself.

"I'm a lamia," he spat irritably.

There were so many chaos creatures to keep track of. Gordon was supposed to make sure she knew things like this, but he'd been useless for anything but making sure that she had access to the trust fund that he'd set aside for her. "What's that?"

"A snake demon. You know, like the ones from ancient Greek myths?"

A hazy memory came back to her of a book with images of a woman with a snake body from when her peers at her boarding school had gone through a Greek myths phase. She almost asked why he was a man, then remembered that the myths humans maintained were rarely the most accurate. Which was exactly why she never bothered to read much human mythology. Shame burned in her cheeks. "Sorry. I don't interact with our kind much. Thanks again for the help. I need to…" She trailed off. *Go where?* The question sank into the pit of her stomach like lead. Isidore had already said her apartment wasn't safe. "Hunters?"

"Yeah."

"Shit." She forced her breathing to steady as her thoughts raced ahead. Gordon had told her not to worry about hunters, because the amulet their people had given her kept the chaos aura concealed. But that was before her sticky-fingered roommate. "I need to get back to my apartment to get my stuff."

"Can you turn invisible?"

"What?"

He sighed and crossed his arms over his bare chest. "I don't know what you are. What abilities do you have?"

"Um...I can fly..." She scoffed. *Obviously, moron.* Taking a deep breath, she started again. "I can detect lies, and control people with my voice...If I'm hurt I can absorb life essence from others to heal...I can use my voice as a weapon. Gold fire magic."

The corner of his lips twitched into a hint of a smile. "That's an impressive list of skills. None of them are going to help you sneak into a building..." He let out a slow breath. "You can stay with me."

Her back stiffened. "I'm not doing that." Long-term proximity with someone had consequences. The recent roommate fiasco was all she needed to remind her of that.

He leveled an incredulous glare at her. "Have any other ideas, Princess?"

She let out an angry, grinding growl.

His head jerked back in surprise. "What the hell are you?"

"None of your business!"

"I just saved you!"

Another wave of dizziness had her swallowing back nausea. She almost told him she was going home, just to be contrary, or maybe to hold on to the illusion of control. But that was a surefire way to get dead. *You cannot go home with a man you just met.* That didn't even cover the half of it. Was he doing this because he cared? Because her magic was luring him in by accident? Her breathing shallowed. She had no other offers. "Fine. Where do you live?"

"Shadyside," he said, naming the neighborhood like it wasn't ironic. "We have to walk to my car, but I can conceal you in shadows. No one will see you but me." Isidore's essence dimmed as his scales transformed back into skin. He held out a hand. "You'll probably turn back as soon as we put some distance between us and the hunters. I swear on the crown of Ninlil herself that you'll be safe with me."

She stared at his outstretched hand. Her instincts screamed to run. This man was a demon, the kind of creature her people were created to destroy. She should run as far away from him as possible. *And go where?* That question reverberated in her mind. She searched his gaze, seeking out any hint of a lie. All she found was concern. What he offered was better than anything Sage and Jayce promised if she tried to get home on her own. She swallowed her pride, gathered her courage, and accepted his hand. He pulled her up, steadying her as she stumbled forward. Their eyes locked. Her heart skipped a beat as the cold in his hands soothed her nerves. Isidore took a deliberate step back, but kept a hold on her elbow as he led her through the undergrowth.

Chapter Four

sidore shut the door to the guest room and leaned his back against it. Through the wood he could hear the door to the private bathroom open, then close. Absolutely nothing about this night had gone according to plan. He'd been approaching Mia's apartment building just as she, Jayce, and Sage had left. He'd followed them to the bar, but confronting them in public was impossible. Mia didn't know him from good or bad, there was no reason at all for her to have trusted him. When they got to the park, he'd thought that he finally had the upper hand. But then Mia had woken up, panicked, and took off through the forest.

He pushed off the door and headed into his bedroom. Walking around without a shirt on wasn't his thing. He grabbed a black tailored T-shirt and pulled it over his head before walking downstairs to the kitchen. It was a pristine white, as if the person who owned it before had planned on starting a YouTube cooking channel, or something. He went to the refrigerator, pulled out the last bag of human blood, then poured it into a crystal glass. His muscles ached from shape-shifting from human form, to demon, to snake, then back again. Not to mention the slashes Mia had left behind in her panic. A quick pick-me-up would solve that problem. The crimson liquid glistened in the crystal, contrasting with the white granite countertops as he swirled it. He sipped like it was a fine wine. There was a hint of frost in the flavor, reminding him of the mysterious winged woman in his guest room.

The glass clinked softly as he set it back down on the counter. His cabal had carefully catalogued and kept track of chaos creatures since ancient times. He had every list memorized since he was a kid. It was part of knowing how to protect yourself. Know your enemies and know your fellows. He played back the moment she'd transformed. The pair of stunning, feathered wings protruding from her back had been otherworldly. They shimmered with every earthen tone at once: brown, orange, yellow, red. The same colors had reflected in her hair—turning it from dark auburn to something breathtaking. He hadn't been able to resist the urge to taste her cheek as he held her to his chest. Spruce, snow, and a hint of sulfur. It had been intoxicating. His fangs ached at the thought of sinking into her slender neck. He wanted to know if she tasted as good as she smelled. If her blood would be red, purple, silver, or even gold. There were so many variants for chaos beings. And then there were her breasts. He'd tried not to look, but Ninmah help him, she was sculpted perfection, right down to the pearled peaks of her nipples.

Knock it off, idiot, he ordered himself as his blood rushed south. *It's just her damn aura messing with your head.* Her voice was also something of a mystery. Hesitant, accented. He couldn't place where she was from. It *almost* sounded Middle Eastern, but not quite. He worked his jaw and rubbed his face. Something felt off about her. A nishutu shouldn't have struggled to transform. If anything, she should be struggling to maintain a human shape. He couldn't imagine trying to keep *that* much chaos contained all the time.

Frustrated, he trudged back up the stairs. A floral scent wafted through the gap around the doorframe and into the long hallway. He swallowed back a moan of pleasure and rapped his knuckles on the door. "Mia?"

He heard a drawer slam shut, followed by soft footsteps. His pulse kicked up for no gods-damned reason. She yanked open the door. His breath caught as he saw her fiery golden eyes for the first time. He hadn't realized she'd been wearing contacts earlier. Her hair hung in damp waves over her shoulder, and it still shimmered. Magic coursed through her, barely contained beneath her skin, which glowed a faint golden hue. He blinked and noticed that she was wearing a pair of his sweat pants and one of his shirts. And definitely no bra. "Do you want something to eat?"

"Do lamiae even eat?"

"Yeah. It won't kill us to eat real food. It just won't keep us alive."

She licked her plump, heart-shaped lips. Without the

lipstick, they were a dusky rose color that complimented the warm, golden undertones of her skin. "I'm starving."

He led the way down the stairs and to the kitchen. "I don't have a lot. Just some crackers and maybe some cheese…I don't entertain much."

"Can we get takeout?" She pressed her lips together, then sighed. "Never mind. I can't get to my money right now."

"I can order us something. Chinese okay?"

"Yeah, that'd be great. Thanks."

He slid his phone out of his back pocket and opened up a delivery app. "Here, you can pick whatever you want."

She took the phone, her expression wary. "You're sure?"

"Yeah. I should have realized you wouldn't want to trust me with food after what happened. Order what you want, then I'll add my stuff to it."

"Thanks…" Her hair fell like a curtain over her face.

He leaned his elbows against the high counter where a line of barstools sat. When she was done she handed the phone back, then he placed the order after he'd added something just so she didn't have to feel awkward eating alone.

Mia sat heavily in one of the stools and held her head in her hands. "I don't know what to do." Her admission was laced with desperation.

Isidore's chest tightened and he shifted uncomfortably. "Don't you have anyone who can help?"

Her hands dropped to the counter and her gaze fixed on a large "Live, Laugh, Love" wall hanging. "I have a bag in my apartment, and enough cash to buy a bus or train ticket out of the city. If I get my things, then I can leave…

Damn it! My students' exams are still on the table." She buried her face in her hands.

Sensing that she was too distressed to be guarded, he decided to needle her for information. "You're a teacher?"

"I'm a doctoral student and a professor of record at Carnegie Mellon."

"What subject?"

"Environmental engineering." Her fingers tangled in her hair. The nail polish that had been so perfect only the previous day was chipped and fragmented. "I have a week and a half until my flight to Ecuador. This couldn't have waited until then?"

He studied the sharp relief of her face, imagining what it might be like to run a finger along her jaw. *Focus.* "I didn't recognize your accent. Where are you from?"

"Baffin Island."

His brows knit together. "What?"

"Canada. An island up north, above Newfoundland. My…" She pressed her lips together in thought. "…people…don't speak English. I learned in school."

Every word she spoke landed like a half-truth. Unease slid down his spine. Newfoundland was Storm Feather territory. His throat tightened. Maybe his father was right, that she was a potential enemy. "Are you with the Storm Feathers?"

Her head tilted and she stared at him like he'd asked the most idiotic question imaginable. "What is that, a college band?"

He laughed dryly as his shoulders relaxed. *She's just a*

woman here to get her doctorate, not part of a conspiracy.
"It would help me a lot if you would tell me what kind of nishutu you are."

She jerked her head to fix her golden eyes on him. When she spoke, her voice had a melodic, sharp quality that was deliciously painful and mesmerizing at the same time. "Isidore, tell me what you're doing following those hunters."

Words were drawn out of him as he leaned toward her. "One of them murdered a cousin of mine. I was sent to help eliminate them."

"Who sent you?" The question was softer, cajoling.

"My father…" He was drowning in golden flames that licked his soul and lit a fire in his belly. "We're a lamia cabal that have operations based in Philadelphia."

"What does your cabal do?"

Her lips looked so soft, like a silk scarf. "We run a hospitality business."

"And what else?"

Her breath was warm on his face. He didn't know when he'd gotten so close to her, but he could see the tiny creases between her sculpted brows. Flawless, beautiful. "We offer exclusive members access to a suite in select hotels, where they're guaranteed a relaxing time. They think they're getting drugs, but it's just where we feed. We have to drink blood and absorb sexual energy to survive. The business is a front. Sometimes—" Something in the back of his mind yanked and he jerked away, shattering her spell. "Aspu's burning balls! What did you do?"

"I'm trying to figure out what you want!"

"I want to help you!"

Her jaw tightened. "Your cabal runs a secret business in Philadelphia, where they suck people's sexual energy and send out members of that cabal to track down chaos hunters to kill them! Why the *hell* should I trust you?"

His breaths were ragged and he took several more steps back. He tried to corral his mind away from his swollen groin and back to the problem sitting in front of him. That, though, didn't help. The problem sitting in front of him was the same woman who was using magic to muddle his thoughts. "All right, yes. We do those things. And yes, we do have a hand in some illegal stuff. For the love of—" He took a deep breath and let it out. "If I wanted to, I could seduce you right back."

Her eyes darkened. "Try it."

Lord of heavens, how he wanted to. "I'm not lying. That really is what I'm doing here. Now your turn. What are you?"

Chaos sparked as their eyes locked in a silent battle of compulsion magic. She blinked, her shoulders hunching forward as she ducked her head. "Lamassu."

Stunned silence stretched. "What in the kur…" He trailed off, and his mouth hung open. "That's not possible. You're extinct."

"No, we holed ourselves up in one of the most remote places of the world. It's hard to hide when your voice causes every human in your vicinity to become a brainless meat sack."

"You're…" He wasn't sure what to say. A part of him

wanted to call her a liar. Lamassu, created by Inanna and Enku. She wasn't just a nishutu—she was a divine one. Made from the primordial waters of Nammu herself in the heavenly realm. His mouth went dry as he tried to keep the undertow of nightmares from drowning him. "Do they know? The hunters."

"No, of course they don't know. I don't make a habit of seeking out sehru or nishutu—it's dangerous. The only reason I talked to Piper was because she caught me off guard by using her phone to talk. And the only reason I'm talking to you is because I'm trapped here!"

The doorbell rang. He swore under his breath and went to get the food and tip the driver. Flashes of memory broke through his walls. The taste of the sukkalu's golden blood on his tongue, radiating magic through Isidore's veins, bringing him back from the edge of kur. He accepted the food and shoved his thoughts back into the vault where they belonged. When he came back, Mia had her head in the refrigerator. His eyes were naturally drawn to the curve of her ass as she bent forward. He suddenly realized why her magic had felt achingly familiar back at the café. It was all too enticing to imagine feeling that kind of energy again. Not just from taking the blood of a divine nishutu—but tasting that holy, erotic energy that he alone could savor. He had to school his face back to something that he prayed passed as neutral as she emerged with a pair of Pepsis.

"I felt like pop." She sat down and slid the second can to him.

"Thanks. Nice use of the local vernacular."

She accepted the container of stir-fried rice noodles and chopsticks. "Pittsburgh doesn't have a monopoly on the word pop. We use it in Canada too."

"Good to know." He slid onto a bar stool. "You said you talked to Piper?"

"The Deaf muse I met at the café. You saw her, brunette woman, thin."

"That's Jayce's wife."

Her eyes darted up to meet his gaze. It was hard to keep a straight face as she sucked the noodles into her mouth and swallowed. "I knew it! She said that her husband was a violinist."

Isidore popped the can of soda and took a drink as he tried to think. He was sitting across from someone who was as close to the gods as he would ever get. *If we had any hope of helping her, he needed information.* The can clanked softly as he set it down. "Okay. I just need some help getting a handle on what's going on here. Why is a lamassu in Pittsburgh?"

"I told you, I'm studying—"

"To be an engineer. I got that." He ran a hand through his hair as he tried to tamp down his frustration. It was like talking to a child. "You said you're from Canada—there must be others of your kind somewhere. Can you go back?"

"No." She said the word slowly, in a haunting whisper, like wind blowing through a cavern.

The hair on the back of his neck stood on end. "Why?"

She ducked her head, hiding her face. "Every one hundred years, there's a ritual where a baby is chosen to become a maru hiptu, a sacrifice." Her voice cracked and she cleared her throat. "My people chose to cut themselves off from the world at least a thousand years ago, but they knew it was important to keep up with what's happening in the world. So, a child is chosen to be symbolically killed and sent to live as a ghost in the wider world. I send back reports every few months—any of us who are still alive do. They're collected and archived by our matriarch. I think it's just me and Gordon now. He's the previous sacrifice, and my adoptive father. We can feel the other maru hiptu, and one died last summer. I never met them. Gordon wouldn't tell me their name."

Isidore gripped the edge of the counter and willed his voice to stay calm even as anger threatened to burst out of him. "They sent you out here without any kind of protection?"

Her eyes flicked up. "I had an amulet that hid my magic and helped keep it contained. It's not very comfortable to wear. I have to take it off at night so I can sleep. My roommate stole it last week when she moved out. I texted Gordon about where to get a new one, but he never responded."

"Aspu's *fucking* depths—are you kidding me?"

Mia startled at the fury in his voice.

His magic swelled and he had to focus to rein it back in. The lamassu were supposed to be divine protective entities, not heartless demons who passed their children through the fire. His cabal was made up of *literal* demonic criminals, and he'd never heard of anyone being this cruel. He took deep breaths. "Do you have any idea what kind of danger you're in without that amulet?"

She shook her head, her golden eyes wide in alarm.

"Nergal's burning pits…" He rubbed his face with his hands. She was utterly alone. No clan. No family. No idea that there were monsters lurking in the dark ready to devour her. *Like me.* The thought winded him. He'd nearly drained Basim, the sukkalu who'd been locked up with him, dry, all because his blood was so powerful. *Would hers taste the same?* His stomach tightened and he pushed the thought away. The Storm Feathers would burn a city to the ground for a chance to claim a lamassu. Other cabals would pay fortunes to capture her. If anyone realized what she was, she'd be *lucky* to end up dead instead of bound to a master who wanted to bend her to their will. "Look. There's more than just hunters out here. My cabal isn't the only demon clan to have gone into the crime business. There's loads of them. Some of them do some shady shit—like capturing nishutu and selling them to the highest bidder at an auction. There's even some human cults that have formed to purge the world of chaos beings for ideological reasons."

Her face drained of color. "I didn't know," she stammered. "Gordon was supposed to tell me this stuff…"

The demon inside him sibilated and coiled at the idea that anyone would abandon this divine princess. His fangs throbbed, aching to mark her, to claim her as his own before anyone else dared to take her. *We are not fucking doing that,* he snapped at the demon side of him. First chance he got, Isidore was going to sink his fangs into this Gordon's throat and rip it out. Any thought of buying a plane ticket and sending her on her way had gone right out the door.

He couldn't let her back out on her own. What he'd told her was just the tip of the iceberg of dangers lurking out there. "You're not leaving this house until we replace that amulet."

The temperature in the room felt like it dropped ten degrees as her expression darkened. Her chaos aura expanded, warping everything around her so it wavered and flickered. "Don't you *dare* tell me what to do! I am a lamassu, not some sehru servant of Aspu!" The pictures on the walls trembled at the sound of her voice.

Holy shit, she's powerful, he thought as he stumbled back. She also had no control. That was a fucking terrible combination. He wasn't a stranger to power, his entire world was structured around coveting it. The strongest survived and the weak were picked off. But this was raw divinity, channeled through someone who had never been taught how to wield it—and that was terrifying. It was a miracle she had survived this long without being found by someone. He averted his eyes, hoping the sign of submission might settle whatever cosmic beast was threatening to burst out. "I'm sorry. You're right. It's your choice. I meant that I'm offering you my home until we can get you a new amulet." He held still. Watching her from the corner of his eye, his muscles coiling as he prepared to dodge any sudden attacks.

Mia's catlike eyes stared, unblinking. Only her shoulders moved with her shallow breaths.

He licked his parched lips. "Mia, just take some breaths. You're in control, not the chaos. Or the beast."

She blinked. There was a snap, and then all the magic got

sucked back into her body. A shiver ran through her, and she shrank into herself. "I don't know what's wrong with me," she whimpered as fat tears rolled down her cheeks.

Slowly he relaxed and took a hesitant step closer. "How long has it been since you've transformed or used magic?"

"Um...I don't remember." She sniffed and wiped her cheek with a palm as she raised her head. "I haven't transformed into my divine self since I left the island when I was eleven. When I use magic, it's just little pieces here and there. I just skim a little bit off the surface."

He raked his fingers through the knotted mess that was passing for his hair. That amulet she had wasn't just keeping her magic hidden, it had made a damn good attempt at snuffing it out completely. Now it was unleashed and she had zero guidance on how to manage it. "Chaos magic has a way of getting restless. You have to use it or you'll explode. Not literally," he added hastily. "But it does get harder to control. You said the amulet helped keep the magic contained?"

"Yeah."

"That doesn't sound safe."

She pressed her lips into a thin line. "You just said that showing my magic is unsafe. Now hiding isn't safe either?"

"Rotting corpses of kur...Balance, Mia. I'm talking about balance." He rolled his neck. "We'll deal with this later. You're exhausted. Sleep. We'll talk when you're not about to set my kitchen on fire. The guest room is yours for however long you want it. I can put the food away for us." He watched as she got up and walked into the hall.

Damn it, this wasn't his problem. He wasn't her guardian. He shouldn't care. But he did. Maybe because he owed the universe a debt he could never repay. Maybe because the gods had thrown a fucking lamassu in his path just to remind him how unworthy he was. Either way, he knew he wasn't letting her walk back out that door. Not alone. Which meant he had to find a local group that would be willing to extend their protection to her. He rubbed his face with his hands. The House of Crimson Fang was only just starting to build tributary networks in Pittsburgh—there wasn't anyone that owed him a favor yet. "Fucking hell," he muttered as he let his hands fall. The only way his father would approve of offering her protection was if Isidore revealed that he'd accidentally unearthed a supposedly extinct species of chaos being. *Definitely not doing that,* he thought irritably. There was no way that road led anywhere good for Mia. *Just deal with the chaos hunters first, then you can work this out.*

Chapter Five

Mia woke in bed, wrapped in the most expensive sheets she'd ever touched, wearing the most comfortable T-shirt and sweat pants she'd ever worn, staring at the plaster medallion above her head. Her gaze traced the intricate petals and leaves of the innermost circle. It looked so out of place among the bland updates the landlords had layered on. The artistic scrollwork and beaded design that surrounded the inner beauty of the medallion was a feeble attempt at protecting its essence.

A dull ache bloomed in her shoulders, spreading outward. Chaos magic pricked at her insides like a thousand tiny needles in response to her racing thoughts. One wrong breath, one stray memory, and it would explode out of her. A low, anticipatory growl came from deep in her soul. Heat pressed behind her eyes. The idea of embracing the cosmic divinity inside of her was terrifying. She'd only fully transformed once, seventeen years ago. It had been a crisp, clear winter night on the island. The aurora borealis shimmered in the sky in vivid greens and blues that darkened even to violet. Something about that sight had stirred the creature inside. It came roaring out of her in an explosion of technicolor magic, and for days she'd trembled in fear at her own power.

Six months later had been her symbolic drowning. She immersed herself in the hot spring that was at the heart of their sacred volcano and emerged as a ghost. Water that tasted of salt, metal, and earth dripped in thick streams down her body. She shivered, naked, as their matriarch stepped forward. Her face was shrouded by an eerie, shadowy veil that protected her from the ghost of the dead girl. A sharp pain shot up her spine as her bones quivered in response to the memory. Mia's breaths grew shallow. "Don't you dare," she muttered as she concentrated on the molded petals above her head. The rumbling magic settled and she relaxed against the mattress. The silence was suffocating, thick as a blanket over her face. It reminded her of that first night at boarding school, when she'd curled under the sheets, alone and terrified.

This is all Gordon's fault! she thought viciously. If he'd done what he was supposed to and actually prepared her for the outside world, then she wouldn't be lying in some stranger's guest bed, mewling like a lost kitten. She rolled over and hugged a pillow to her chest. There wasn't any way to contact him now. How many nights had she spent staring at the stupid location app on her phone as he did gods knew what. The infuriating crimson pin taunted her as it bounced across the United States, Canada, and Mexico.

Once she'd watched him go on a whirlwind trip to Europe over the course of a few weeks. *Pathetic,* she chided as she buried her face in the down pillow. Even if she got her phone back, her adoptive father wasn't going to respond.

Unable to tolerate lying in bed even a second longer, she sat up and slipped her feet into a pair of plush guest slippers before quietly padding out of the room. She cracked open the door and listened. A soft, even hissing came from Isidore's room. She slipped through the door and crept down the stairs that led to the large, open-concept bottom floor. The kitchen gleamed as a pink-hued dawn light filtered through a small window above a metal sink. Her stomach growled. She went to the fridge to pull out her leftovers from the night before. Then froze, staring at the half-eaten container of rice-noodle stir-fry. The last thing she needed was to get drugged again. *Isidore wouldn't do that,* she retorted to the paranoid thought. Her chest tightened as indecision gripped her. The lamia hadn't told her a single lie in their entire conversation, and, while he had used mild seduction magic to get her to admit to being a lamassu, it hadn't been nearly enough to override her autonomy. *If he wanted me dead he'd have killed me while I was asleep.* She grabbed the container and shut the fridge with a decisive *thunk,* the cold metal handle slick under her fingers. One by one, she yanked open drawers until she found the cutlery.

As she ate, she meandered around the first floor of the upscale town house. She passed under a beam that marked the separation between the living and kitchen area. There was a sleek 4K television in the living room. In front of it was a long feather-gray couch. She let out a quiet laugh. It was like the owners had watched too much HGTV and made the aesthetic of every single room based on one of those house-flipping shows. The entire house was like an overly decorated shell, but the inside was empty.

She scraped the bottom of the container, then stopped. Across the room, tucked into the corner, stood an electric piano. Her brow rose as she set the empty container down on an end table next to a vase of roses. The last time she'd seen a fancy electric piano was in undergrad. She walked over and ran her hand along the smooth edge under the keys until she found the power button. It clicked on, and the display screen came to life. A giddy energy took over as she pulled out the cushioned bench and sat down. This thing put the cheap Yamaha keyboard at her apartment to shame. She pressed down on middle C and jerked back as it blared out the note. Panicked, she frantically looked for the volume control and turned it down. Her heart pounded in her ears as she listened to hear if Isidore had woken up. Even with her superior hearing, she couldn't detect his breathing from all the way upstairs, but there was no sound of footsteps. She pressed the key again, then relaxed when it played more softly.

The giddiness sent tingles of magic into her fingertips, a dangerous thrill. She ignored it. Just this once, she wanted to play without the potential consequences of a human hearing her sing. She couldn't pass up the chance to soothe away the hot fear that still clung to her after everything with Jayce and Sage. Her fingers pressed down on the keys. Slowly at first, then faster as Evanescence's "My Immortal" poured out of her. There was a kind of malicious satisfaction in playing a song by an artist who was known for writing exaggerated pieces after Jayce's smug arrogance. She sang the lyrics with her most haunting voice. It filled the open space. The magic inside her blended with the vibrations and the curtains on the wall shivered as if brushed by an imperceptible breeze. She floated, suspended in the harmonization of music and magic until the air shifted. Suffocating, electric. The song died in her throat. A prickling dread crawled up her spine, her instincts screaming before her mind caught up

"That is stunning."

Mia slammed her hands on the keys as she jumped up, sending the piano bench crashing to the ground. A man loomed beneath the ceiling beam, towering over her. His eyes were a stormy blue that peered out beneath a pair of thin brows. His dark hair contrasted sharply with his pale ochre skin. He smirked as if he'd just won a game Mia had no idea she was playing. "Nice voice."

A raw, guttural scream split her throat. The man recoiled and slammed his hands over his ears. Paintings on the walls vibrated. The vase of roses shattered, sending water cascading over the edge of an end table. Roses scattered onto the ground, thorns mixing with glass shards.

A thud from upstairs. Then pounding footsteps. Isidore flew down the steps, skidding to a stop as his gaze snapped to the stranger. The shadows in the room quivered and darkened as he fixed his glowing green gaze on the man. "Germund, what the *fuck* are you doing in my house?!"

Chapter Six

sidore's heart pounded in his ears. Mia stood frozen, her face locked in terror, her skin shifting with unnatural, liquid color. A sickness twisted in his gut. She was unraveling, seconds from losing control. Her hair had turned light auburn with streaks of earthen orange and yellow, and her golden eyes glowed like the sun. There was no telling how massive she might become if she shifted into her chaos form, or what she might destroy when she did. He snapped his attention back to the bastard who'd taken him prisoner. Who'd beaten him, starved him— then locked him in a room with Basim, hoping the hunger would turn him into a monster. The one who wouldn't hesitate to kidnap Mia and sell her to the highest bidder, or just keep her to fuck with him.

Germund lowered his hands and held them in front of him, palms facing out. "I thought the Crimson Fangs liked to keep out of nishutu business. Or is the protective nishutu a *private* investment? You never struck me as the type to take on a tributary whore." His irises swirled like storm clouds as they turned a deep blue-gray.

"That's none of your business!" Isidore hissed, striding across the room without taking his eyes off the anzu. He planted himself between Mia and his unwanted guest. "People usually send a text to let someone know they're stopping by—especially at six in the *fucking* morning!"

"See, I thought that when you lamiae played with your food, it was in a sex dungeon, not a fancy rental," Germund drawled, his smirk widening. "Did she taste good?"

Isidore let out a rattling hiss. *Calm down. He broke in to get the upper hand on something. Figure out what it is.* He rolled his shoulders. "What do you want?"

"You're hunting a woman named Sage Halloway. I'm hunting the same woman. Instead of tripping over each other, why not work together? Unless, of course, you'd rather have the Storm Feathers take the credit for cleaning up your mess?" His eyes slid back to Mia.

Isidore's skin rippled as his demon rose to the surface in a knee-jerk protective wave. Onyx-and-green scales erupted, covering every inch of him. "Eyes here, or I walk."

"Isidore…" Mia's voice came out low and chuffing, like an animal ready to pounce. It sent a primal shiver up his spine. "Who is this?"

Before Isidore could think of a reply, Germund cut in, "Germund, an anzu nishutu and the heir to the Storm Feather Creed. Isidore and I spent a lot of time together last August."

The chaos magic coming off the three of them sparked,

making the table lamp flicker. Isidore focused on the feeling of the wood floors on his bare feet. He didn't want to add fuel to this tinderbox by rising to the bait Germund was trying to lure him in with. The *last* thing he wanted to do was partner with him. "I don't see how I benefit from this."

"You know, in a more civilized time, you'd have offered me coffee so we could discuss the deal."

Isidore's lip curled. "Fuck off."

Germund smirked. "The huntress you're after went rogue from her clan. She's from one of yours—clan Venator Mons. They've got base operations in Appalachia."

He could feel Mia's searing gaze on the back of his neck. There were going to be a lot of uncomfortable questions he'd have to answer after this. At the same time, relief washed over him. Finally, he had some concrete proof that Sage was the rogue hunter from Venator Mons. "What's her objective?"

"They rejected her as a full member because she was born without magic sight. She got pissed, then vowed to come back and challenge their leader when she'd gathered all the chaos she needed."

"Where'd you get the information?"

"Shook it out of the leader. Unlike you soft-bellied snakes, we're not scared to get a little rough." He pulled back his lips, showing off gleaming silver teeth that could rip the flesh right off living prey.

Mia's shoulder brushed his, and energy sizzled through his skin like static before a storm. He could feel her trembling, but kept his feet planted, and his gaze stayed locked on the anzu. It was idiotic that the most dangerous thing in the room was a terrified woman with a child's-level knowledge of what was happening. He wrestled his thoughts back to Germund's words. If Sage didn't have magic sight, then that explained Jayce. "The man she's working with—he has the sight?"

"Yes." Germund crossed his arms. "Here's the deal. You kidnap the muse, we use her as bait, and then I'll take them out for you."

Before Isidore could reply, he was smacked by a wave of searing heat radiating from Mia. Magic surged around her in jagged, blinding streaks.

When she spoke, it was a deep-throated snarl. "Touch Piper and *die!*"

Germund moved into a defensive stance, poised to strike if she so much as twitched.

Sweat dripped down Isidore's back as he turned to face her. He didn't doubt for a second that Mia would rip them to pieces if she thought they were a threat to the muse. "Mia, take a breath—"

Her attention snapped to him. "Piper is marked for divine protection!"

He slowly lowered his eyes in submission. The demon inside him hissed in protest, but he tamped down on it. "Okay." He turned his attention back to Germund.

The anzu's beady storm-blue eyes darted between the two of them.

Isidore needed this encounter to end. Germund already knew too much about Mia. "I'll rescue the muse. Then we can *ask* her if she wants to participate in the downfall of her captors." He held his breath.

Mia's anger lowered to a simmer.

"If that fails, we can always use your pet here," Germund replied cooly.

Isidore's fangs extended. His vision blurred with fury, and his demon slithered through his mind, itching to strike. "Not on your life!"

The minute the anzu's lips curved into a smile, Isidore knew he'd given him exactly what he was looking for. Germund's gaze drifted to Mia. "You sound like you're far away from home, pet."

"I'm from Canada! And don't call me that!"

Isidore hissed in frustration. He could see interest lighting up the man's eyes. Canada was Storm Feather territory. It wouldn't take him long to sniff out the lie. His demon coiled, whispering in his ear. *End him now. Rip out his throat before he can take her away.* He let out a slow, controlled breath, forcing his muscles to relax. Murdering the next leader of the Storm Feathers was a surefire way to start a war. One the Crimson Fangs weren't ready for.

"Interesting." His triumphant smile was laced with malice. "Isidore, to answer your question about why I want to team up with you. Naturally, I wanted to check in. There's been talk that you've lost your edge." He grinned as Isidore's fury simmered. "As I said, my thought was to try to get the muse. Your talents are better suited for sneaking into a human residential building. Lightning going off tends to make a scene. I've linked eight kills to the hunter—"

"Eight?" Mia gaped. "How have eight people gone missing and no one's noticed?"

Germund crossed his arms as he studied her. "They have…That's why I'm here."

"I meant by the authorities," she snapped.

Isidore worked his jaw, trying to remind himself that she was new to their world despite being at the top of its hierarchy. "A lot of chaos beings live off the grid, or they're connected to a group. It's rare to find someone living entirely on their own. Hunters focus their efforts on people who don't have ties that might call the authorities if they up and disappear." Unease wormed under his skin. She was the exact target these hunters would choose. Easy to pick off.

Germund pursed his lips in thought. Then a smile slowly crept across his face while his dark eyes stayed cold as ever. "I had a hunch you were the mark. I knew they'd moved to the area for a reason." Germund turned to Isidore. "Your Daddy will wring your neck when he finds out you're risking his reputation for a stray." His arms dropped to his sides. "As a present for your participation, I'll let you keep the muse and stay quiet about your pet here. So that Daddy doesn't get too mad."

Mia's aura pulsed, expanding outward in a wave of gold heat. The floor vibrated.

Isidore glared at the anzu. He was baiting her on purpose, and Mia was too out of control to notice. Germund's jibe about his father reminded him what was at stake if his father found out he'd disobeyed and directly involved himself with Mia. Isidore would be forced to abandon her, and Germund would snatch her away in the night and do gods knew what with her. He let out a slow breath. Working with Germund kept him close enough to watch, and gave him a way to eliminate the hunter. He could tell his father the strike team wasn't necessary because an opportunity presented itself and he'd handled it. That didn't help him figure out what to do with Mia, but one thing at a time. "I will liberate the muse, *ask* if she wants to help, then we go from there. We'll have to do something about the bodies once they're dead," Isidore reminded him.

Germund ran his tongue over the points of his teeth.

Mia blanched.

Isidore grimaced. *Subtle*, he thought in disgust. "We'll work it out later. Now get out of my house."

"I need your number. Just to keep in touch, since you seem to eschew visitors."

Isidore glowered as he gave over his encrypted number. Nothing in the heavenly or earthly realms could convince him to trust Germund with his real number. With the business out of the way, he escorted Germund to the door and slammed it behind him. "Stay gone, bastard," he muttered.

His body stayed frozen in place. He'd just agreed to work with someone he *knew* couldn't be trusted. At the same time, he wasn't in a position to bargain. Germund was *much* more powerful than him. He was older. Had more contacts. The smart thing to do would be to call his father and tell him that there was a complication. But then he'd have to explain Mia.

A thin whine floated on the air. His racing thoughts came to a screeching halt and he rushed back to the living room to find Mia on the couch. She looked like she was trying to smother herself with a pillow. Her skin still shifted and changed colors, and he had to look away before he got motion sick. He tried to focus on calming his breaths. Adding fuel to her panic wasn't going to help anyone. "You okay?"

She jerked her head up, blinking flaming gold eyes that were rimmed with red. "I can't make it stop," she whimpered.

"Make what stop?"

Her lip trembled. "My divine essence…I hear this roaring in my head."

He stuffed his hands into the pockets of his sweatpants as he tried to think. Basim's divine essence had drawn him to interrogate Isidore, to determine if his soul was destined for damnation. Mia was a protector, though, not a holy arbitrator of impassive judgment. Following that logic, the way to provoke her divinity would be to threaten her charge. "It's your connection to the—to Piper," he corrected quickly.

"He'll hurt her."

He took uneven steps closer to her. "I won't let that happen. I wasn't lying when I said I'd rescue her."

"I know…" She wiped her damp cheeks with the heel of her palm. "Why did he say that you could have the muse?"

Her voice was distant as she repeated Germund's words. Isidore hiked up his shoulders, like the movement would help him keep his guilt locked down. *Of course that's the question she starts with.* He'd expected it, but that didn't make it better. "Because one of the seedier things my cabal does is chaos being trafficking. Usually we only deal with umamu—the kinds of creatures that you can't have a conversation with. Like...Minotaurs, or a hydra." He grimaced as he forced himself to continue. "We have deals with some hunter groups. In exchange for leaving us and our allies alone, we *very rarely* hand over a muse, or other less powerful sehru."

Mia was so still she almost looked like a statue.

Blood rushed in his ears as agonizing seconds ticked by. He'd just admitted to a being created to execute divine punishment, that he had corroborated in trafficking. Finally, he couldn't take it anymore. "I know it's not pretty."

"Is this it?" Mia's voice was barely above a whisper. "How all of us live? Sehru, nishutu—hiding, hunting, selling each other out?"

His face burned with embarrassment, like it was somehow a personal failing on his part that their kind had to resort to violence to scrape by. "Kinda, yeah."

"I understand why my people cut themselves off, and why they think of the maru hiptu as dead. Our leaders must know it's just a matter of time before someone kills us. We're alone. No family. We can't make real friends because talking to humans is a nightmare and our magic interferes." A tear rolled down her cheek. "I can't even replace my godsforsaken amulet."

Aspu's balls, he thought irritably. Sighing, he sat heavily on the ottoman in front of her. "It's not all bad. Most sehru and nishutu live under a patron. Safety in numbers, and all that. You swear fealty, you pay your dues, and you get left alone. Those that don't either stay small enough to avoid notice, or they get picked off. Humans do terrible shit to each other all the time, we're not that much different. Except that we live under a shadow anarchy instead of a proper government."

She stared at him like he'd grown an extra limb. "A reasonable person would call that apocalyptic."

"This *is* the apocalypse. The time of myths is over. Humans won. And the rest of us? We're just trying to survive."

Chapter Seven

Hot pressure built behind Mia's eyes, provoking tears that threatened to flow down her cheeks. She wanted to take Isidore's words, tear them to pieces, and then light them on fire. Instead, they burrowed deep, taking root in the shadowed soil her people had tilled when they killed her. She should have known. Only an apocalypse could drive a society to such desperation that they'd leave one child to die every hundred years.

Die.

You're already dead, she thought bitterly. *They just didn't give you a grave.*

But she wasn't dead. Every sip of her too-expensive wine, every walk through the park or new song she sang was a testament to the fact that she was still very much alive. "I didn't fight to survive only to be killed all over again," she whimpered.

Isidore's expression softened, and his arms relaxed at his side. "There're ways to survive."

She shook her head, unable to find the words that would convey her emotions. "You said everyone already has families, or groups. You also said that hunters look for people like me who don't have ties. Even with a new amulet, someone will find me eventually." Grief like she hadn't experienced in years crashed over her. There wasn't any point in sitting here and taking up his time. He already had a family and cabal to look after, he didn't need some stray kitten that hadn't even learned to retract its claws yet. She threw the pillow to the side and stood up to leave. "I don't belong here. I'll pack up and disappear. It's what I was meant to do, anyway—"

Isidore's hand shot out like lightning. Icy fingers wrapped around her wrist, anchoring her in place. Soothing cold fanned out from his touch, dousing the golden fire that burned just beneath the surface of her skin. "Mia," he said in a low, steady voice. "Sit."

His touch weighed her down and she followed his lead, keeping her head ducked so she could keep some modicum of dignity. She was supposed to be stronger than this.

"I told you that you can stay with me as long as you need to."

"You don't live here."

He blew out a puff of air. "I *do* travel a lot. My father—he's our leader—mostly uses me these days for stuff like what I'm doing here. Investigating potential threats to the cabal. I'm not just going to abandon you here when I leave. There's other sehru living around here. Some of them are even stand-up people."

She picked at the decorative fringe along the edge of the throw pillow. There was a question she had to ask, but she wasn't sure she was ready for the answer. "Why are you helping me?"

"Aspu's *depths*—I don't know." He stood and planted his hands on his hips as he paced the length of the couch. "There was a situation a few months ago. A trade dispute between two patrons. They needed a neutral broker to oversee the transfer of what I thought was a sehru." He stopped and turned to face her.

A shiver ran up Mia's spine. The brightness in his eyes dimmed, like a flame choked by the rain.

He licked his lips. "We were contacted by two tributary clans. They were trying to arrange a trade with each other, but their relations were lukewarm at best. I told you my cabal doesn't usually deal in chaos being trafficking. It's not because we're good people, it's just that it puts a target on your back. The sehru turned out to be a divine nishutu—a sukkalu."

A memory stirred in the back of her mind, and fragments of a story she'd heard as a child came back in threads that refused to weave together. "What's that?"

"They're another divine chaos being. They're a rare chaos being that doesn't have a chaos form. They were meant to act as judges and condemn the wicked." Only his shoulders moved as he took in a breath. "I was part of the team helping to ensure a peaceful transfer. When we arrived at the rendezvous, we were ambushed by the Storm Feathers. Germund captured me and the sukkalu. We were held captive together. I didn't know it at first, but they had offered the sukkalu a deal that if he helped get useful information out of me, then they'd let him go. I'm not the heir to the House of Crimson Fang—that would be my sister—but I still am an elite member. In order to stop me from escaping, they..." His voice cracked, and he cleared his throat. "There's sigils you can use to bind up the inner cosmic form."

Her hand moved absently to her neck where the amulet used to sit. "My amulet had something like that..."

"They didn't waste money on an amulet. They just—" His jaw flexed. "They carved them into my skin."

Mia's breath caught. His voice felt like an abandoned cave, hollowed out eons ago by a long-dried-up river. He didn't look at her. His fingers twitched against his thigh before he closed them into a fist. She swallowed against the tightness in her throat.

He sat next to her on the couch, keeping his eyes fixed on the floor as he leaned his elbows on his knees. "Sorry, this is gruesome. Anyway...I told you human food can't sustain us. They starved me for a long time. I got delirious...They did some other things. The sukkalu couldn't stomach it. I was at the gates of kur, and he snapped. He offered himself for feeding in exchange for helping him escape..." His voice was hollow. "I couldn't turn down the offer. Nishutu blood is powerful. There's a reason everyone's after it—including some lamiae. I was starving, and desperate..." He swallowed, gaze fixed on the floor. "It wasn't a full feeding, just blood, but because he was divine it gave me enough strength that I fought our way out. I don't know when the sukkalu died...They were holding us in this cabin just over the Pennsylvania border. I stole a car and by the time I looked in the backseat the sukkalu was dead."

Mia had no idea what to do. He'd just admitted to killing someone. Or, at least, admitted that his actions somehow led to a divine nishutu's death. Isidore was a demon, a creature her people were born to defend humanity against. But there were so many missing shards of his story. She couldn't watch him rip himself apart from the inside for a crime he wasn't even sure he committed. Her fingers hovered, uncertain, before she finally reached out and took his hand. She hummed softly. Golden light passed through their connection, wrapping around his wrist, then up his arm. He looked up at her sharply. Thin tendrils of gold slithered into his green eyes, warm as dawn light. Slowly, his shoulders relaxed.

"You really do sing beautifully," he murmured. "I heard you, from upstairs."

"I didn't mean to wake you."

"I'd die happy if I got woken up like that more often."

Her face warmed.

Isidore almost smiled, then his expression faltered. "It took a few months for me to recover from...everything. When I was sent on another assignment, I got spooked. My father took me off the more...um...active side of our dealings, and moved me to intelligence. That's why I'm here." He let out a breath and his shoulders sagged. "When I saw you at the café, I could tell that you were a protective nishutu. I followed you home because I knew in my gut those hunters were after you. My father told me to let you deal with it…" His fingers laced with hers. "I couldn't do it…My plan was to warn you, then help you get out. I was at your apartment building when you suddenly up and left. So I followed you instead. That's how I found you at that park. You weren't passed out for very long. Whatever elixir they used to drug you didn't take into account that you're powerful."

She couldn't take her eyes off him. Not a single lie had flowed from his lips. A small part of her recoiled in disgust at the story. He didn't say it outright, but he'd obviously been part of the *active* business for years before the incident. She might not be the most street-savvy person, but she'd watched enough mafia movies to know what that entailed, even if they weren't accurate. Isidore might be helping her, but he'd killed before. Was willing to passively participate in chaos being trafficking. Yet he hadn't kicked her out when he realized how little she understood of the world, and he'd backed her up when she refused Germund's suggestion of using Piper without her consent. Even when it would have been the easier choice to let Germund do what he wanted, given that Isidore must have been terrified facing down his tormentor again.

Mia let out a breath and rubbed at the pressure that had begun building in her eyes again. She'd thought she could hide behind the ivory towers of academia, or in a remote field lab somewhere, but the world the gods had abandoned them to truly was apocalyptic. There was no escape. She had no friends to turn to. Isidore wasn't a good person, but he wasn't all bad either. He didn't deserve to be starved and tortured.

Mia let out a breath. "I'm sorry you had to go through that...I really do appreciate you explaining how things work to me. It must be like having a nagging kid around."

His grip on her hand tightened and he offered a weak smile. "It's not that bad." Long moments passed as they gazed into each other's eyes. "When I asked if you had friends, you said no...You really don't have anyone?"

Her chest tightened. "I've never been alone per se. There's always someone to talk to. Someone who likes me. That's what the alluring aura does. It makes people want me around. Humans are sensitive to it." She laughed sadly and looked down at the throw pillow's orange-and-red spiral design. It was similar to the mandalas in those coloring books some of the people in her cohort liked so much. From a distance, it looked like a tangled mess, but up close you saw that there was both precision and art to the seemingly chaotic. "They're not really my friends. I could tell them that I was going to blow up the fountain at Point State Park and they'd still think I was charming. Not even the monotone voice on my app was enough to keep them away. Once I wised up and started using American Sign Language, all bets were off. You could probably crown me queen of the Deaf community—and I'm not even Deaf. How messed up is that?"

"What about other sehru or nishutu?"

She gave a one-shoulder shrug. "My people might be

hermits, but they've got egos the size of icebergs. They claim that lamassu are the greatest of the divine nishutu because Inanna and Enki purposefully created us as divine enforcers. One of the few tidbits of advice Gordon gave me was to stay away from other chaos beings, because they all were only out for themselves." Her breathing quickened to a ragged, uneven pace. She'd always thought his comment was because he hated the world. Now she saw that his words had been a warning. *The world likes to break pretty things, Mia.* That's what he'd said once. The words expanded, swallowing her whole. She felt like she was suffocating.

Slowly, as if afraid of startling her, Isidore cupped her cheek and brushed away a tear with his thumb. "Mia…"

She turned her head sharply to the side. "I'm sorry…I just…I need some rest. I didn't sleep last night." Without stopping to take in his expression, she was on her feet and hurrying up the stairs as more thick tears rolled down her face. She fell against the door to the guest room and jostled the knob until it opened and she tumbled inside.

"Mia!" Isidore ran up the stairs.

She slammed the door shut and turned the ancient lock that probably didn't even work anymore. Tears streamed down her face as she backed up into a chifforobe. The old-fashioned wooden wardrobe rattled against the wall. She slid to the ground, pulling her knees to her chest.

"Mia, I'm sorry," he called through the wooden door.

Her throat was too tight to reply. She sniffed and pressed her forehead to her knees.

The doorknob jostled, then stilled. A beat of silence

stretched as he hesitated. Then the door swung open. His shoulders were squared, his hands balled into fists at his sides. He didn't step across the threshold. "I didn't mean to push the boundary. You're my guest, I didn't invite you here to—"

"That's not it," she stammered as she tried to wipe away the tears with her palm.

"Then, what?"

She shook her head. There weren't enough words in English or any other language to explain how she felt.

He slowly lowered himself into a poised crouch. "What do you need?"

A pause. Then her lip quivered. She knew what she needed. Something no one could give her anymore. But his gaze held hers, and the words slid off her tongue in a whisper. "A friend."

Frantic heartbeats passed.

A muscle ticked in his jaw. He exhaled. "Okay." His voice softened. "I'll be your friend."

A fresh wave of tears poured out of her. Isidore was up and across the room before she could blink. He gently pried her wrists away from her knees and drew her to his chest. She didn't have the strength to fight against his offer of comfort, so she clung to him, sobbing until her muscles ached. He stayed solid and unmoving, as if he could absorb every shaking breath, every broken piece of her. Then, softly, he hummed. A lullaby of warmth and quiet magic, of something safe. She wrapped her arms around his torso. Magic danced and bobbed in rhythmic spirals. A sense of calm draped around her. The tears slowed, then stopped. His gentle hum continued, lulling her into sleep. Her eyelids became heavy.

"Mia," he whispered gently in her ear. "The magic isn't why I like you."

The last of her energy drained away, and she welcomed the soft winter of his touch as she drifted into a dreamless sleep.

Chapter Eight

sidore tapped his head against the chifforobe as Mia slept peacefully in his arms. There was a gentle heat pulsing from her and it warmed his icy skin. The whiplash—from her music, to her screams, to her meltdown—left him feeling like raw sinew stretched to snapping. The one time he'd let himself feel something real, and he'd made her cry. He took a cleansing breath. *It wasn't you, she's just overwhelmed.* Her entire world had shattered overnight. She was lost, hunted, alone. He couldn't imagine how that felt. His family might be fucked-up, but if chaos hunters were after him? He wouldn't be left at the mercy of a stranger. Plus he had a handful of close contacts outside the family he considered trusted friends.

And yet, Mia hadn't hesitated to throw herself into Piper's fight. A fight she had no reason to believe she could win. She barely knew the muse, but the second she had sensed Piper was in danger, she had marked her for protection. Like she couldn't do anything else. The thought made his chest tighten.

His demon let out a low, quiet hiss, *And she's ours to protect.* He reflexively brushed away the possessive thought. Mia was a divine protective nishutu, created by the gods to act as their envoy to defend those who deserved it. His soul was so tarred over, you could probably just light him on fire.

Still...he wasn't imagining it, was he? There had been an undeniable pull between them. Maybe it was just their magic, colliding and amplifying into something neither of them could control. But the feeling itself was real, right? He held on to her more tightly. Since he'd been old enough to think about dating, his father had made it crystal clear that he would be choosing Isidore's future partner. It would be a partnership that served the family's political agenda. Mia was not a good tactical partner. Having a divine nishutu around would draw unwanted attention that could put the entire House of the Crimson Fang at risk. But if he shielded her, wasn't that already a claim? It was effectively saying that she was his. His problem, his responsibility.

He stared at the crown molding. Mia would never swear fealty. She wasn't like the tributaries who sought protection from the Crimson Fangs in exchange for loyalty. Wasn't like the elites who married for political advantage. She wasn't even like a proper lamia partner, sworn into the family like a well-bred acquisition. She was feral, untamed, a divine creature meant to roam free. Lamiae sought subservience at every turn. There was no way she'd ever fold to his father's whims. He was ruthless. She was divinity.

A small ember of light glowed inside the icy blackness of his soul. If a lamassu could harbor even a pinch of affection for him, that meant he couldn't be all bad. Right? He glanced down at her. There was a soft parting of her lips as her breath sent a tingling of warmth on his neck. It was the most relaxed he'd seen her. *You've known her for less than a day,* he reminded himself as he again leaned his head back against the chifforobe. That thought didn't quench the building desire. The demon inside him slithered, restless, hungry. His family had talked about the way their demons felt about their partners. Possessive—dangerously possessive at times. The demon didn't care if Mia wanted him or not. She was *his* lamassu. His. And if anyone touched her— he'd kill them. *Territorial bastard,* he thought, disgusted. But the demon didn't care.

He stayed on the floor until his back ached from the carved, decorative trim on the wooden furniture piece digging into him. Gingerly, he shifted his grip, gathering her close before standing. She weighed nothing in his arms, but the moment felt impossibly heavy. She stirred as he laid her down, a soft whimper escaping her lips. His throat tightened. He brushed a hand over her hair, trying to soothe her. Mia's movements calmed, and her breathing evened out once more. His feet felt like they were planted to the floor. Even if she could probably annihilate him with a single blow in her—what did she call it? He wracked his memories. *Divine essence.* A smile spread on his face. It was such a poetic phrasing. Anxiety pushed out the affection. Powerful or not, she was vulnerable. Germund knew she was here, and thanks to Mia's verbal slip, the anzu also could at least guess she was divine. He had already proven he could sneak into the house. Knew she was from inside his own territory and was an unknown, potentially dangerous threat to him. If she belonged to a family, or a tributary, she would be shielded. But Mia was alone—a walking invitation to predators like Germund, to hunter clans, to every desperate nishutu lord looking to breed power into their bloodline. She was worth more than gold, and she had no idea.

Isidore's arms flexed at his side. There was no way he was leaving her alone. He swallowed as his gaze drifted to the space next to her on the bed. It was entirely too easy to imagine slipping in beside her. That warmth she generated was better than any drug he'd ever tried. The demon inside him shivered in quiet rapture. *Oh, fuck no.* He deliberately turned his back to her and walked to the bedroom closet where the landlord had a spare blanket stashed.

When he'd set up his makeshift bed, he lay down and stared at the plaster medallion on the ceiling. The beige paint made it hard to appreciate the detailing the sculptor had put into the flowers at the center. Beneath the layers of neglect, it was still there. Still beautiful. Just waiting for someone to see it, to bring it back to life. Warm affection bloomed in his chest as fatigue dragged him into sleep. No matter what it took, he'd see his lamassu safe. And when she was ready, he'd help her find a home.

~

Something warm prodded at his arm. Isidore groaned and blinked to find himself gazing at a pair of radiant golden eyes, and he was submerged in the smell of sulfur and pine. For a moment he thought he was still dreaming. Pressure built between his legs as his gaze fell onto her plump lips. Then everything crashed down on him. Heat surged up his neck. He dragged a hand down his face, willing his body to calm the fuck down. "What time is it?"

"It's sunset…"

His brain lagged. Sunset. That meant…He groaned. "Shit, I overslept."

"I didn't want to wake you. I wasn't sure if you normally slept like that during the day, or…"

"I'm not a vampire."

Her sandstone cheeks darkened in a flush. "I know, I just…didn't know…"

He couldn't suppress his chuckle. "Don't worry about it. I don't know specifics about most other chaos beings." Groaning, he got to his feet and stretched his arms over his head. "Was there enough to eat?"

She stood and tucked a strand of hair behind her ear. "I ate your leftovers. Sorry."

"It's fine. I ate my own food last night while you were taking a shower."

"What?" Her eyes widened.

He smirked. "I brought supplies with me. Some blood I got from a dealer." Though that bag of blood had been the last. He was going to need to solve that problem at some point. As if on cue, the scent of her enticing fragrance hit him like a drug. It grew with each fluttering beat of her heart as it pumped her warm blood through her veins. His fangs ached, sharp and insistent, his stomach twisting in protest at his restraint. He took a deliberate step back. "We stop for food, then your apartment. Get in, get out, no mistakes."

"We're going now?"

"Yeah. With the pit stop, it'll be well after dark. We sneak into your place first and get your things. Then we wait until the right moment to get Piper."

She pressed her lips together as she hugged her elbows. "I can't talk around humans."

His groggy mind struggled to figure out what she was trying to get at. "Okay…" Slowly, it dawned on him. She'd said that humans were susceptible to her voice. Sirens had a similar problem. Her phone was how she communicated if someone didn't know sign language. *And her phone is with the hunters. Perfect.* He ran his fingers through his knotted hair. "I'll give you my phone. We'll download the app you need. Just let me get ready."

As soon as she left he went to the master bath attached to his room and ran a cold shower. He tilted his head back as the water ran down his body. It was a bizarre oxymoron. His body always ran cold, yet he felt like he was on fire. He wanted to know how Mia thought, what she dreamed about, what she would sound like if she laughed without restraint. He smiled faintly as he thought about her voice. Hesitant, with an accent that was unique to her. His stomach twisted. This wasn't hunger, or lust. It was something he'd never thought the gods would let someone like him feel.

He imagined what it would be like to have Mia in here with him. Water would bead and roll down her smooth skin, dripping off the points of her hardened nipples. Her head would tip back, exposing the elegant column of her neck as he kissed her. He would press into her, feeling her life pulse beneath his fingertips. Ripe, ready.

Fuck no. He jerked himself out of that imagining. There was no way in hell he'd put her at risk like that. A feeding was intense. *You're just hungry.* It had been over a month since his last proper feeding. That hunger drew him back into his imagination. Kissing down her jaw, and grazing that soft, vulnerable neck with his fangs. His venom would have her melting in his palm, trembling, aching, whispering his name. He could take his time, savor every gasp, every shudder. Heat would pool between her thighs, and he'd be there to draw her deeper. Her energy would spill over, thick and golden, a buffet ready to be devoured.

"Isidore, are you ready?"

Her voice was a jolt to the sense. *Don't fuck your food,* he reminded himself. That was a dark road with no map. "Yeah! Just a second!"

Quickly, he finished his shower. But even after he dressed, the tension in his chest didn't ease. He rolled his shoulders, trying to ignore the ache under his skin—the warning sign that he needed to feed soon. *You can find the dealer tomorrow and get more blood,* he thought as he went to meet Mia at the bottom of the stairs. She was wearing another pair of his sweatpants and a T-shirt. Both concealed her feminine frame. *Good,* he thought as he strode toward her and grabbed his keys and wallet from the basket by the door. His hand hovered over a magically locked cabinet where he kept his knives. Giving himself a shake, he opened it with a wave of his hand and retrieved a folding tactical knife. "Ready?"

"Yeah."

Isidore unlocked his phone and handed it over. "Download what you need." He watched her out of the corner of his eye as he started the car. It was impossible not to admire her strength. Even now, as she was running headfirst into danger she wasn't trained for, she didn't hesitate to problem-solve. She'd made reckless choices, sure, but none of them had been thoughtless. Mia was inexperienced, not foolish. With some time, she would be using that analytical mind to do some serious damage to her enemies.

He took a breath and let it out through his mouth. "We're going to your apartment first. You can get your things together. Then you're going to wait for me."

"But—"

"No. You wait." He glanced at her, then back to the road. "I'm serious, Mia. I need to make sure it's clear. If it's not, then we hold out in your apartment. The only reason I'm taking you is because you can communicate with Piper to keep her calm."

Mia huffed and crossed her arms over her chest. "Fine."

The tension drained out of him. "I'm sorry, I didn't mean to talk down to you. What we're doing is dangerous, and you're not trained. If things go badly I want you to run."

"I can't leave Piper."

"Mia…"

"She's my responsibility!"

"Aspu's depths…" A muscle spasmed in his jaw. "You're the more valuable target for them. If this goes badly, it will tip them off that Piper means something to you. They won't hurt her. We can regroup and try again." His grip tightened on the steering wheel as he waited.

Golden wisps of magic came off her in waves. Finally, the gold subsided to her usual earth-tone aura. "Thanks… I'm sorry I dragged you into this."

"I dragged myself into this. Now let's get you something to eat."

~

By the time they pulled up to the apartment building it was fully night. Isidore parked a few blocks away, in case the hunters were keeping a lookout. He gripped the steering wheel as his heart quickened. Every instinct in him was screaming to get her far away from this place.

"I can feel her more clearly," Mia's soft voice cut into his thoughts. "She's nervous."

"Hopefully we can fix that." He opened the car door and relaxed in the cool spring air. There was a digital clicking sound, and he glanced over his shoulder as Mia walked around the car.

She held up the screen, now set to dark mode. Are you okay?

"Yeah." He reached out to her and gently pulled her

toward him by the elbow. "Hold on to me. It'll be easier to keep the shadows close."

She fit against him like they were made to move together. *Not the time.* He pushed aside the pleasant buzz of magic that came to life between them, and focused. There wasn't a soul on the block. The shadows hugged their bodies like a thin veil, covering them on three sides as they made their way down the street. He led them to the back entrance of the building.

"Wait here," he ordered. He allowed the demon to rise to the surface. His bones cracked, then shifted. Pain rippled out in waves of pinpricks along his muscles. Scales replaced skin. Clothes dissolved as he writhed and sank to the ground. Mia gasped softly as the shadows receded. He flicked his tail in satisfaction and slithered in a dramatic serpentine motion so the light hit his scales. A shiver rippled down his spine. He tasted something heady, something unmistakable—Mia's desire. *Later,* he thought. Slithering into a hole in the wall, he popped out in the basement and found a space open enough for him to shift back before opening the back door. He grinned down at Mia, making a grand sweep with his arm to welcome her inside.

She took the lead as they found the back stairwell. Every muscle in her body was tense—like a wildcat preparing to pounce. She stopped at each landing, tilting her head to listen. It was fascinating watching her. He'd wondered if she had enhanced senses of some kind, like his sense of smell. *I should have done research on lamassu before we did this,* he thought. But between tracking the hunters and keeping

Mia alive, there hadn't been time to sit down and properly look into it.

Finally, they reached her floor. He sidled past her and shimmied his shoulders out the door to make sure the way was clear. Satisfied when he was met with an empty hall, he opened the heavy, fire-resistant door wider for her to pass. He hovered over her shoulder as she fumbled with the keys to the apartment. Her hands shook as she turned the lock and pushed the door open. They hurried inside and he shut the door behind them.

Mia froze. His gut twisted as he peered over her shoulder. The place had been gutted—blankets, DVDs, nail polish bottles were strewn across the floor. Someone had been looking for something.

He put his hands on her shoulders and leaned down to whisper in her ear. "Don't move. I'll check it out."

She nodded.

He moved around her and into the main area, his instincts sharpening. No scent of intruders. No lingering traces of magic. Whoever did this was long gone, but that didn't mean they hadn't left something behind. Slowly, one step at a time, he swept through the apartment. He pushed open the door to her bedroom and grimaced. It was the worst room by far. Papers, books, journals, and pens encircled the space around her desk. The mattress was overturned. A strong perfume permeated the air, and he scanned the ground until he saw a shattered bottle of something.

"I don't understand…"

Isidore jumped as Mia appeared beside him. He rubbed

his face as he willed his racing heart to slow down, and made a mental note that she could stalk silently. "They were looking for information about who might have helped you, I'm guessing. Was there anything here that would give them information about you?" He knew this wasn't Germund. The man was a devious son of a bitch, but he wasn't messy like this.

She didn't respond. Her expression was vacant, as if she weren't really present.

Shit. He raked his fingers through his hair. His carefully laid out plan was crumbling before they'd even gotten started. Leaving her alone in the apartment like this wasn't an option. She was too out of it, and he needed to assess the damage. The biggest risk was that the hunters had found out what she truly was. "Mia, did you have anything like magic papers, or communication devices back to your people?"

"No…" Her fingertips trailed the pattern of wedges and lines inked on her wrist. "They tattooed a marking on me. There's an incantation I use, and I can dictate my messages for our matriarch to collect…"

His gaze flicked to the tattoo. He'd noticed it at the café, but with everything going on he hadn't stopped to really *look* at it. It felt similar to Mia's magic, although he could tell she wasn't the caster. The magic flickered with a pale violet energy. *That's not normal,* he thought as he took a step closer. Their surroundings blurred as his mind focused. Something felt off about her people's entire process. There were too many points of failure. Starting from the fact that they left children defenseless, although that was remedied by having the previous sacrifice raise them. "What happens if you don't send back reports?"

Her head jerked up. For a long moment, she just stared at him with wide, anxious eyes. She licked her lips. "Once I was a few months late and I started to get vivid night-mares...They went away when I sent in the report."

A shiver ran down his spine. This wasn't just exile, or some archaic tradition. What Mia described was active enforcement using psychological manipulation. Dread crawled across his skin as he saw her situation for what it was. Her people hadn't just exiled her as a ghost, they'd bound her to them in forced servitude. It was brutal. Cold, tactical. *It's a war tactic.* The thought hit him like a knife to the heart. It wasn't that different from how his father handled cabal business. If he ever stepped too far out of line, there would be consequences. What Mia's people had done was wartime intelligence. A closed-loop, self-sustaining surveillance network designed for maximum efficiency with minimal risk to the homeland. It was a system that never required open warfare. Never required resources. Never required its people to fight. Instead, it outsourced all of the risk to a handful of agents who had no support, no reinforcements, and no escape. Choosing children meant they were too young to question the system, or fight back. They would seamlessly integrate with human society, and their divine natures were chained down with that disgusting amulet they gave her. She still thought of herself as a sacrifice, a ghost, an agent with a duty. But there was nothing holy about this.

Mia's voice broke the silence. "If I had stayed…"

The horror still writhed beneath his skin, lined with burning fury, but this moment couldn't be about his rage. He could let himself get angry later, after he'd gotten her safely back to his house. He wrapped his hand around her wrist and crushed her against his chest in an embrace. "You're going to be fine." He kept his voice low and commanding, so it would chase out whatever fears were getting a foothold in her mind. Her frame trembled against him. "I'm not going to let anything happen to you or Piper." His grip loosened and he pulled away to look into her face. Her cheeks glistened with tears. They didn't have time to unpack how truly awful her people were. She needed to move. To keep surviving. "Do you have a duffel bag or anything?"

She blinked as she processed the question. "My emergency bag is under the bed." She didn't move.

He gave a curt nod, releasing her so he could search around the bed until he found a packed weekender bag. The sight of it, already prepared, made his stomach tighten. How long had she been waiting for something to go wrong? Because even if she didn't admit it out loud, she clearly had thought about it. He exhaled slowly, gripping the strap a little too tightly before slinging it over his shoulder. "You said your students' exams are somewhere?"

She nodded.

"Can you show me?"

Her eyes blinked once. Twice. "Yeah…" She turned and glided out of her room like a spirit.

He followed closely behind. The dining room table was

miraculously untouched. When he peered down at one of the exams, he was met with a string of indecipherable mathematical nonsense. It was almost funny that the hunters probably had the same reaction he did, and ignored the documents. He set the duffel down and collected the papers.

"Thank gods they didn't get these..." She took the stack from him and stuffed it into a backpack. "I'd be screwed out of my job...my visa..."

He watched her sadly. "Is there anything else you want to get? Any personal items? When the hunters are dealt with, we can come back."

"Um...The only thing I really have that I care about is a stone..."

"A...stone?"

She averted her gaze and fidgeted with the strap of her backpack. There was a long pause as she composed her response. "It's already in the duffel. I picked it up as Gordon escorted me off the island. We're not allowed to take anything with us. My things would have been burned at my death... There was a smooth, glasslike stone. I found out later it was obsidian. The island is part of an archipelago above the Arctic Circle." Her shoulders relaxed as she rambled. "Obsidian is formed when lava cools rapidly. It prevents crystals from forming. You find them all over the island, since obviously it's freezing up there most of the time. It's not as bad in the summer. There's hot springs inside of some of the caves in the volcano. It's where—" She clamped her mouth shut. "Never mind. This doesn't matter. I'm just rambling."

His heart twisted and he stepped toward her, then took the backpack out of her hands and put it on the floor. "I like learning about you...What's your native language?"

Her eyes flicked up to meet his and there was something fragile hidden in her gaze. A hesitation to open up. His stomach tightened. How many people had she told about her past? How many people had cared?

"It's a dialect of Akkadian...I've never talked about my people before. Not one word in seventeen years," she said softly. "Actually, this is the most I've ever spoken. It's a wonder my voice still works. I guess it's the singing. I'm sure my English pronunciation is terrible. I used to hide in the forest to practice..."

His body moved before he could stop it. He pulled her into him, arms locking around her. For a split second, she was stiff. Then she melted against him. His demon hissed in satisfaction. He pressed his nose into her dark auburn hair and took a deep breath of that intoxicating smell of the cold tundra. No words passed between them. Slowly, they made their way to the couch and she curled up into his chest. He felt himself molding around her, making space so he could hold her closer. This was the type of affection that was almost unheard of in his family. Lamiae were passionate, and wild. What Mia needed and offered was softer, gentler. A kind of caring that you couldn't find from a demon. He hadn't realized how his father's cold indifference had left him hollow. His very nature softened with her around, and the ache in his chest, the one he hadn't even noticed before, finally began to ease.

Chapter Nine

Mia gripped Isidore's polo shirt in her fist. The mess of the apartment felt like walls closing in around her. She felt like she was suffocating. Then he gently stroked her hair. One muscle at a time relaxed. A strange, deep, rumbling purr started somewhere in her throat. The sound startled her. Her mother used to purr like that. When Mia was scared she would climb into the furs her parents shared and her mother would engulf her in a warm, rhythmic purr to chase away the darkness.

"Is your divine essence a cat?" Isidore asked quietly.

"Something like that." She didn't have enough space in her mind as she sank deeper into contentment. "That feels nice."

"Good. Just tell me what you need and I'll do it."

She should have been terrified by that promise. It was one that countless humans had made when they tried to vie for her attention, and was usually a warning signal that she needed to put up more barriers. Instead, it felt nice to be taken care of. To be wanted. Her purr rumbled, and deepened as she considered what it would be like for him to touch her in other places. Heat rose along her collar and up her neck. She'd just met Isidore. The emotions being stirred up were just a result of the magic.

But what if it's not?

The quiet thought came from the back of her mind. Her heart skipped a beat. He wasn't human. That fact had been evident since the moment she'd laid eyes on him in the café. They could resist each other's alluring magic. She lifted her head. Her gaze drifted to his lips. The curve of his mouth. His bottom lip was full, enticing. The dangerous tilt of a smile that promised things she wasn't ready to admit she wanted. The air crackled and hummed. She lifted her eyes and met his intense, electric green gaze that shone with an inner luminescence. Shadowy, opalescent green and indigo danced around him as he leaned closer. His aura wrapped around her like a dark tide, a sharp contrast to the fire rising in her core. His lips hovered over hers, a question, a temptation. Then he leaned forward. A shiver ran down the length of her spine as their lips met, and goose bumps spread in a wave. Isidore took a sharp inhale through his nose as his arms encircled her, trapping her in his embrace. His tongue teased, and she parted her lips. Heat surged as he brushed his tongue against hers. He brought a hand to her face, cupping her cheek as he pulled away. Slitted, snakelike eyes gleamed dangerously. A thrill ran through her. No one in her life had ever looked at her like this. Like she was the only person in the world. She wanted more.

Leaning forward, she pressed her lips to his in a claiming kiss. Golden sparks danced with shadows. He moaned as she deepened the kiss, and his hand drifted down her back, along her waist, then up…She gasped as he cupped her breast and a jolt of ecstasy coursed through her veins.

"Mia," he whispered just before his lips caressed her ear.

Her back arched as he kissed her neck. She wanted to let go, to give in to this. *Would it be so bad to trust him?* Isidore was possessive, the exact thing that had led her to give up on dating. But it wasn't just his possessiveness. It was the way he touched her. Gently, reverently. She gasped as his lips brushed her collarbone. This wasn't just her alluring aura, this was real.

Magic snapped, like a rope fraying all at once. The moment shattered. A sickening pull wrenched through her chest. Piper's panic, sharp and consuming. Mia gasped, reeling as reality slammed back into place.

His breaths were shallow as he dragged himself away. "What?"

"Piper. She's upset." The divinity inside her expanded, flooding her thoughts. All she could think of was that her charge was in trouble, and she was sitting here daydreaming. She was on her feet and running toward the door.

Isidore overtook and blocked her path. "You can't just go running off!"

She bared her teeth. "Move!"

"No. Take a beat. You're letting your divine essence take control."

Claws extended. Every ounce of her attention was

focused on that fluttering, frantic feeling in her chest. Blood rushed in her ears as she waited. The built-up energy sparked in golds, reds, and oranges along her skin.

"Explain to me how that connection works," he said slowly.

She blinked in confusion, reining in the tempest threatening to break free. "Why?"

"Because talking will help you focus."

A flicker of doubt cut through the haze of protective instinct. Was he trying to be helpful, or just slow her down? Years of habitually answering questions had words cascading out of her. "I'm not sure, I've never marked someone before. It's like I can feel when she's scared or needs help. Like she's calling for me."

He let out a voiced sigh. "Okay. Get your bags. We're dumping them by the stairwell on their floor so we can make a clean run for it if we need to."

She grabbed her things and followed him into the hallway, then into the back stairwell. They raced down two flights of stairs. Isidore took her things and stashed them in a crevice created by a large pipe and the wall.

"Stay here, please? I'll get inside, unlock the door, and get you if I can. You're the only one who can explain things without Piper panicking."

Mia nodded. The sight of his shift was both horrifying and mesmerizing. Bones realigning, sinew twisting, human shape dissolving into a viper coiled on the ground. He flicked his tongue, tasting the air, before vanishing into the darkness like a living shadow. *How much time did he spend stalking this place?* she thought nervously as she wrung her hands together. Seconds ticked by. A minute. Finally, there was a faint creak of a door opening. Then footsteps. She tensed, preparing for a fight. Isidore poked his head in and gestured for her to follow. The bright hallway was jarring after the smothering safety of the shadows. But she pushed forward, pulse hammering, every sense on edge. They entered the apartment, and he closed the door softly behind them.

"It's empty," he whispered. "Other than Piper."

She wanted to point out that whispering when the only person there was Deaf was pointless. But the relentless tugging had her rushing toward one of the bedrooms. She tried the handle only to find it locked. Isidore came up beside her, gently moving her aside. He braced his shoulder against the door. Magic crackled. With a grunt, he broke the lock with brute-force strength. Mia pushed past him into the cluttered room.

Piper was a statue, barely breathing, knuckles white as she clutched a sketchbook to her chest. Her wide, haunted eyes darted between them. Mia could feel the weight of Piper's terror like a stone sinking in her gut. Her brown hair hung limply, as if it hadn't been washed recently. A glint of metal caught Mia's eye and she scanned the space around her charge until she spotted a metal chain and locked anklet.

Mia forced her hands to steady and signed, "It's Mia, from the café. This is Isidore. We're here to get you out."

Piper's chest rose and fell in quick, shallow bursts. Mia

could almost hear her heart pounding. Then, slowly, hesitantly, Piper nodded.

Mia sensed Isidore's rising anxiety but ignored it. She walked closer to the muse. "I'm a protective nishutu—your protective nishutu. Can I come closer?"

The sketchbook dropped to Piper's lap. Her hands shook as she formed signs. "They'll be back soon. I can't get the lock."

Mia quietly voiced Piper's words.

Isidore strode to the bed and knelt to inspect the chain. With his bare hands, he yanked. His arm muscles bulged, and he grunted with the effort. The chain links bent, then broke apart. "There...Come on, time to go." He took Piper's arm and yanked her to a standing position. "Get your shoes."

Mia quickly signed his words when Piper's terrified, wide eyes found her. The muse looked frantically around, then grabbed a pair of flats from a pile. Isidore ushered her out of the room as Mia brought up the rear. They froze as footsteps came from the hall outside. Mia held her breath, too scared to even breathe. The footsteps halted outside the apartment.

Isidore hissed and dropped Piper's arm as he took a defensive position in front of them. "The second they come through that door, I want you two out," he whispered.

Reality crashed down on her. She was about to be thrust into a fight. A real one, where she could die. The door handle jerked violently. Then *boom*. The door slammed open.

Sage strode inside as her lips curled into a snarl. Chaos magic crackled in the air. "You really thought you could take her from me?" Her voice dripped with venom as power vibrated around her. "I knew you tied yourself to that bitch."

For several long breaths, no one moved. Fighting was dangerous. The neighbors could call the police, someone could see a spell go off.

Sage's hand moved to her pocket. Isidore was on her like lightning. Hissing, fangs fully extended.

Jayce's hand shot inside his jacket. Mia's attention snapped to him. A pistol gleamed under the overhead light, aimed at Isidore. Time slowed down and the colors of the room shifted. She could see the intricate details of the gun. The strands of Jayce's dirty-blond hair fluttering as he aimed the weapon. The muscles of his hand. His jaw was tight, eyes locked onto the lamia. His finger tightening on the trigger—

Mia moved before she could think. Her teeth lengthened. Claws erupted from her fingers. She charged at Jayce, tearing through his jacket and into his flesh. He let out a sharp yell and staggered back. His free hand shot out, and he slammed his fist into her throat. Mia gasped, then Jayce used his shoulder to barrel her back into a bookcase. Pain exploded at the back of her skull. The world tilted sideways. A sharp corner of a book jabbed into her ribs as hardcovers rained down.

A reverberating bang rang in her ears.

Piper shrieked in terror. Mia's vision swam as Isidore bent forward with a hand pressed to his side. Black blood oozed from a wound.

Sirens wailed, growing closer. Mia lurched to her feet and careened toward Isidore as he stumbled.

Jayce aimed again. Isidore let out a snarl. The shot cracked through the air and Isidore jerked sideways as the bullet grazed his shoulder. Mia jumped toward Jayce before he could get off a third shot. Jayce pivoted. Mia's mind stuttered as her gaze locked onto the gun. Aimed at her. Ready. Isidore's banal, deep, rattling hiss filled the space as he seized her wrist, yanking her out of the way just as a third shot went off. She felt the air compress as the bullet whizzed past her. Flashing blue lights streaked across her vision.

Distant shouting.

Footsteps pounding.

Her pulse was a frantic, erratic drumbeat.

Sage shoved Piper into the back hallway, grip iron-tight on her wrist. "You're not going anywhere," she spat.

Isidore half lead, half dragged Mia through the apartment door, then to the back stairs. They had seconds, maybe less, before police stormed the building. She snatched her backpack and duffel on instinct, barely breaking stride as they hit the stairs. Then they were outside, running. Shadows converged, shielding them from view of anyone in the building who might be watching. They ran through the gaps in the surrounding houses.

Isidore collapsed against the car door, sucking in sharp, pained breaths. Black blood seeped between his fingers, staining his shirt. He yanked the door open and leaned against the frame.

"I can drive!" Mia blurted out without thinking of who might hear.

He glanced at her. His eyes were dull and glassy from pain. Nodding, he braced himself against the hood of the car and made his way to the passenger seat as Mia threw her bags in the back. The moment he was in the car, she pressed the ignition button. Her hands were slick with sweat. She gripped the wheel, knuckles white. She hadn't driven in a year—could she even do this? Isidore let out a low, ragged groan. Mia's spine straightened. She put the car into drive and punched the gas.

～

She drove the entire way back to Isidore's rental with a death grip on the steering wheel. Her hands ached by the time she reached the town house and parked in the driveway. She whipped her head to face him. The deep black stain had spread across his ribs, soaking through his shirt like ink, and giving off a smell of smoke and charred flesh that stung her nose. "Isi…" she choked, her throat raw with fear.

"Just…get me inside…" he muttered through gritted teeth.

Her fingers fumbled with her seat belt and she tumbled out of the car before hurrying to his side. She got his arm over her shoulder. Mia's surroundings blurred together. They were walking to the door. Then she was struggling with keys.

"Upstairs," Isidore wheezed.

She kicked the door closed with her foot and stared, wide-eyed, at the steps. Her back sagged under his weight as his legs gave way. There was no way she could carry him without tapping into her divine essence. She called it forward, and the raw power thrumming in her veins flooded her limbs with inhuman strength, her vision sharpening, the world tilting into a strange, golden clarity. It felt like waking up. She adjusted her grip, then swept Isidore up in her arms, and walked upstairs with heavy footsteps. The door to his room, the farthest down the hall, was ajar. Each step felt like an eternity. Until finally, she was by the bed and gently setting him down.

She knelt between his legs, her breath coming in short, ragged bursts. "I don't know what to do," she whispered, voice trembling.

Isidore's hand brushed her cheek and he lifted her chin. "I'm not a human. This won't kill me, trust me. I've had worse."

"Do you need anything? Is there blood for you to drink in the kitchen?"

"No. I drank the last of it yesterday. You need to lock the doors. I've got fully charged ward stones. Set them…" He took a rattling breath and his eyes blinked slowly. "Set them around the doors and lower windows. Keep you safe. Until I'm better." His hand dropped to his lap as he lay down on his back.

She felt like a weight was crushing her ribs into dust. He'd said that blood was how his kind regenerated. How they survived. Her heart hammered as she remembered his story about the nishutu he'd drained when starving. If a divine nishutu brought him back from the brink of death, then surely her blood could help him. It was better than watching him lie in agony for days, while he drained himself of his magical reserves. *You could die.* Her breaths turned shallow. Swallowing, she steeled her courage. *I am a lamassu. We do not let people suffer if we can stop it, especially people we care about.* She licked her parched lips. "What about me?" she whispered.

His head snapped toward her, and for a moment, there was nothing human in his expression. His pupils swallowed the green of his irises, expanding into endless black voids. The shadows around them seemed to shift and writhe. "No."

"You can just take what you need—"

"It doesn't work that way."

She refused to back down and let him suffer. "You said you don't kill the humans you feed from."

His gaze raked over her, slow and methodical, like a predator judging the tenderness of its prey. His forked tongue flicked out between his elongated fangs, tasting the air between them. Her heartbeat quickened in response. Something stirred inside her. A shadow that sent a shiver down her back. She wondered what it would feel like for him to drink from her.

His lips parted, and at first no sound came. Then words slowly formed, building on one another in his low voice. "Lamiae are not vampires. We're seductive demons. Our essence is sustained on blood and lust. It's never just simple feeding."

"Then, how…"

"Do we do it?" He shifted. Pain flickered across his face and he clutched the sheets in his fists. "The hotel...extra services for guests. They think it's a kink service...I'm not human. I don't just take. I make things...mine."

Her stomach clenched and heat pooled in the space between her legs. She was all too aware that she was leaning toward him. "What do you need?"

"Mia..."

"I asked a question."

"Gods above...Are you asking because of that divine urge to protect, or because you want to?"

She sucked in a breath as an embarrassed heat brushed her face. Was this just instinct? Her entire life had been shaped around protection and sacrifice. How much of that was her instead of an ancient edict dictating her thoughts? Her fingers laced together in an anxious knot as curiosity seeped out of her like vines seeking sunlight. "I want to."

He let out a thin breath of air through his teeth. "Don't offer again until I'm done. There's rules. First, when we feed, the demon part of us is in control. And it doesn't like to hear the word no. If you're given instructions, you do it."

Her mouth was as dry as sand. "Okay."

"Feeding isn't just about blood, Mia. My demon thrives on more than that. It draws power from arousal, from the pleasure of its prey. The more pleasure, the more energy is built up. *You're* a treasure to be cherished. It doesn't want to hurt you, it just wants your..." He swallowed as his eyes trailed down her neck. "Arousal. I feed off it."

She should run. The thing looking at her wasn't a man,

it was a monster cloaked in silken darkness. And yet, his voice had a dark tendril wrapping around her, drawing out something primal. She wanted him to touch her. *Inanna, help me.* She sent the silent prayer to the goddess of love and war who fashioned her. "Anything else?"

"I have to take enough blood to heal…But mostly I need to stimulate you into a frenzy. It's intense. Mia, you don't have to—"

Desire, dark and alluring, unfurled from the shadow in her soul. Heat pulsed in her belly. She wanted to know what it would feel like to have his cold skin against her golden fire. His hands between her legs. On her breasts. After a lifetime of being invisible, she was ready for someone to see. "Isidore…" Her voice was a thin whine. "Take me."

Chapter Ten

leeding walls of kur, Isidore thought as he gazed into Mia's determined expression. He could smell her rising anticipation, desire, and arousal. The demon within him stirred with excitement at the thought of drawing in her sexual essence, eager to finally sink his teeth into her delicate skin and get another chance to taste divine blood. No lamia on the planet could resist an open invitation like this. But she wasn't some random prey he met off the street. This was Mia. His lamassu. His divine princess. He couldn't turn her down, it was too delicious. Enticing. But he had to make sure she was protected from his own dark essence. His usual prey begged for the chase, the pain, the brutal satisfaction of being claimed by a predator. They paid money for it, wanted to be presented to their master. Silent, bound, waiting until that moment his venom had them careening into pleasure. But Mia wasn't here to be conquered, or controlled. She was a gift from the gods giving herself in offering, and he couldn't hurt her. Not like he'd hurt Basim.

He pushed away the thought of the dead sukkalu and wracked his brain. There *had* to be a way to protect her from the insatiable appetite of his demon. He spit out the first thing he could grasp. "Pick a safe word. It can be anything that won't come up in normal conversation. If you say it, I'll stop. My demon wants your arousal, not fear."

Her throat bobbed as she swallowed. "Obsidian."

His pulse roared in his ears. It was a good choice. One he'd hopefully be able to hear and honor. "Have you ever had sex?"

She shook her head.

A pleased hum came from his demon. *Not going to happen,* he snapped at it. When he made love to her, it was going to be soft, and gentle. Not something to get his demon off. "That's fine. I don't have sex while feeding. Have you used sex toys? A vibrator?"

"Yes."

The quiet little mew drew his demon closer to the surface. "Can I use them?"

Her eyes were wide, her smell only intensifying everything inside him. "Yes."

"Finger play?" Anticipation built, crowding out the pain, as she flushed. "If you don't say no, I'm taking it as a yes."

"Okay," she whispered. "No seduction magic."

His demon curled its lip, but Isidore pushed it aside. "No magic, although my venom is an aphrodisiac. It will make things more…intense. I'm not going to hurt you, but I'll test your limits. You have to hold still; if you can't, I'll have to restrain you." He tried to think of other logistics around the pain and hunger. "You say that word, Mia, and we stop. Any time. Immediately. You're my princess, and my demon's treasure. We value your body, mind, and soul. Ready?"

The soft, sensual curve of her lip quivered. Her golden eyes were bright with nerves. Then, after what seemed like an eternity, she gave a tiny, almost imperceptible nod.

He dug his nails into his palms, forcing himself to focus on the present. Her breathing, her golden eyes. *Stay in control.* But then her scent hit him like a tsunami, and the world tilted. The air crackled as the magic within him stirred. Green and indigo swirled in a chaotic tempest. Desire ran wild, untethered as his restraint crumbled. The demon coiled inside him, whispering, urging. *Why fight? Why wait? She's offering herself, isn't she? Take her. She's yours.* "Come here."

Slowly, she scooted closer. Isidore reached for her, and seized her forearm. *No, slow down,* he ordered. But the demon's impatience blurred into his movements and he dragged her roughly into his arms. He brought her wrist to his lips, and flicked out his tongue, tasting the salt of her sweat, the faint musk of her need. Her pulse was warm and alive beneath his fingers. The demon lunged forward and he sank his fangs deep into her flesh. Hot, thick liquid teased his tongue. Sulfur, frost, salt, and pine flooded his senses. The aura around her intensified. He reveled in it. Revered it. His princess was delectable. His grip tightened on her wrist, pulling her closer as he absorbed that precious life of hers.

His grip on her tightened as his strength trickled back.

The torn flesh expelled the bullet that had lodged in his gut before melding together. The pulse beneath his lips drummed wildly, singing for him. He told himself to stop. He was going to stop. But the demon shredded through his restraint, howling with need. His grip on her wrist flexed. She gasped, her balance slipping, her body tumbling into his lap—exactly where she belonged. "Beautiful…" he muttered as he caressed her silken, soft face, carefully avoiding the scratch above her eye. With tenderness that bordered on obsession, he scraped the tender column of her neck with the points of his fangs. He needed to fill the emptiness inside him with her essence. The lines between morality and demonic, dark desires blurred. The demon hummed in satisfaction, a low, reverberating sound rattling in his chest. His hands kept moving down to her shoulders. Her supple breasts. His grip tightened, his hunger expanded.

"Did it—"

His voice shifted, deeper, darker. "Don't talk unless you're spoken to." The words slipped out instinctively.

Her body tensed in his arms.

He almost curled his lip in frustration. Prey didn't talk. Prey kneeled, prey waited, prey obeyed. But Mia wasn't kneeling. She wasn't gagged. She was watching him, thinking, choosing. *Slower, gentler,* he ordered himself as he ran a fingertip along the length of her angular jawline. "Yes, kitten. Your blood was exactly what I needed. But it's not all I need." Gods, how he'd been playing over what he would do to her if she ever agreed to open herself to him. "I'm going to strip you bare, and make you beg for me to bring you release." He reveled at the shiver that ran through her body. He took the hem of her shirt and drew it up.

Her hands moved to help.

"No. You're mine now. I decide what you wear—or don't."

She went still, every muscle tense.

His brow furrowed in concentration. Usually, his clients would shudder in anticipation. He breathed in, tasting her nerves. There was a flicker of resistance behind her golden eyes. *Not a client,* he reminded himself. He had to be careful. If she shut down now, he'd lose her. He continued to draw up her shirt, revealing her full, soft breasts. He longed to caress them, massage them. *Not yet,* he scolded as the tiny part of him that could still think logically tried to rein in the feral beast. He let his hands fall to her hips. If he were stronger, he'd stop now. Take the offering of blood and leave. But her pulse was decadent, her alluring magic a magnetic pull. Suddenly he knew, with chilling certainty— he was going to devour her. "Stand up.""

She hesitated, but at his firm thrust she unfurled her legs and stood between his splayed knees. He hooked his thumbs into the elastic band of her sweat pants and panties, pulling them down slowly as if she were a present to be unwrapped. His fingertips brushed down her thighs. Her breath hitched and he smirked in satisfaction. It was all exactly as he imagined. Her standing in front of him with everything out on display. He could smell the venom starting to work. But she was a long way off from reaching her peak arousal, from satiating his hunger.

He stood and took her wrists, bringing them together by her naval. Keeping them secured with one hand, he let the other play with her collarbone. His gaze moved to her neck. One day she'd wear a collar for him, so every lamiae would know that she was his. But not yet. Tonight he would teach her what it meant to be coveted by a demon. "Come with me." He tugged firmly on her wrists, pulling her off-balance.

"Where—"

"I told you not to talk unless spoken to." He kept his voice low. Talking blurred lines, and that wasn't something he needed while he was walking along the edge of his self-restraint.

She followed his lead, her eyes wide, pupils dilated.

He led her to a chaise. "Kneel on it." His demon didn't wait for her to comply. It wanted her where he could see her. All of her, so he could play with his treasured prey. He couldn't stop himself from placing a splayed palm on her sensual, round ass, pushing her up onto the chaise. Dropping her wrists, he adjusted her chin. Her arms.

She leaned away.

"You stay where I put you." He adjusted her again, forcing her knees wider apart. Tilting her chin so he could see exactly where his next bite mark might go. "Do you want me to tell you all of the things I'm going to do to you tonight?"

"Yes," she whispered.

He gently stroked her hair. "First, I'm going to blindfold you." The scent in the air shifted as her body responded.

Hunger urged him on. "Then I'm going to touch you. Should I tell you where?"

"Yes…"

He let out a slow hiss of amusement. "You'll have to wait and see." He made quick work of getting the silk blindfold from among the things he'd brought with him. None of it was what he'd prefer. His kitten shouldn't be subjected to hand-me-downs, even if he did meticulously clean them. He was going to buy toys just for her one day. They would be tailored to fit her body, to maximize her pleasure and accentuate her beauty. Leaning forward until he was almost touching her, he tied the blindfold securely, then stepped back. Her entire body was quivering, stoking his ego. His impatience had him wanting to lean in close and skim the rising sexual energy radiating from her. He reined it in. There would be more than enough of her to sustain him for a long while if he waited.

"Kitten, I'm going to touch you." He focused on the rise and fall of her shoulders. Then delicately traced his fingers across the tops of her breasts.

Her breathing quickened.

"Did you like that?"

"Yes." She leaned toward him.

"Don't move."

Every muscle tensed at once, and she froze in place. "What am I supposed to do?"

He realized that forcing her to comply with not talking would be impossible without resorting to a gag. That was only going to make her panic, which wouldn't get her where he wanted her to be. "Nothing. You wait until I give you what you need. Do you want me to touch you?"

She licked her dusky lips. "Yes."

He rewarded her with a stroke across her stomach. The muscles bunched, and rippled. His hand trailed down her thigh. "Sit back on your heels, knees spread."

"Why?"

This was impossible. He hooked an arm around her waist and pinched her pearled nipple between his fingers. She yelped and tried to get free, but he held fast. "I told you the rules."

"I can't follow your instructions with you holding me," she snapped.

A sharp correction would've worked on a client—pain was their pleasure. But if he punished her, he might lose her. He exhaled through his nose, forcing himself to let go of the impulse. He needed to teach her, not break her. Wrapping both arms around her thighs, he hoisted her up. She yelled in surprise and toppled over his shoulder. He walked to a wooden chair by a desk and dropped her into it. Leaning forward, he caged her in. His eyes half-closed as he got a wave of her intoxicating emotions. "Do you want to find out what I have planned?"

"How could you have planned this? You were bleeding out not ten minutes ago."

"Since the moment I saw you, I've been wondering how you'd taste." He leaned in close, nuzzling her neck. "You smell like frost and sulfur. I can't get enough of it. Should I tell you what I want?"

"What?"

"Demons love to corrupt. It's what we're made for." That was what he'd been taught to want. But the thought of breaking Mia didn't thrill him. It made his stomach churn in disgust. "I don't want to corrupt you, kitten," he murmured, stroking her auburn hair. "I want to worship you."

Mia's breaths were shaky. He watched the flicker of uncertainty cross her face. She was still assessing him, deciding. *Not a client to be dominated,* he reminded himself. Then she leaned back, her body wary.

The demon quivered in triumph. He'd caught his divine kitten, now it was time to play with her. "Good girl. Don't move."

Chapter Eleven

Mia tracked Isidore's footsteps, each one a quiet thud against the wooden floorboards. The blindfold was infuriating. It made her all too aware of Isidore's venom surging in her veins. Everything felt too sharp. Heat pooled in her core. She should rip it off. One tug, and this would be over. No more mystery. No more uncertainty. But…did she want that? A shiver ran down her spine. Dark curiosity gripped her, luring her further into his games.

A cold hand brushed the back of her neck and she startled. "Put your hands out to your sides."

Gods above, what is he doing now? Hesitantly, she dropped her arms. She jumped as he tied a silk rope around one wrist, then the other. "Isi—"

"You'll call me 'prince' when we're in my world."

She swallowed and startled as he tightened the rope and secured it. "I can't move."

"That's the point, kitten. You can't be trusted to hold

still when I tell you to." He circled around to the front. "Spread your legs."

"I'm scared." The admission came out as a thin mewl. She felt pathetic. Stupid. *Why did I agree to this?* Her breathing grew shallow as panic set in.

"Shh." He ran his fingers through her hair. "Do you want to stop? You just have to say the word, and this ends."

She'd almost forgotten. The tension in her chest loosened. This wasn't real. It was a role-play, like the dark things she'd heard about in undergrad. Control was hers to give, hers to reclaim. She wasn't powerless, she was choosing this. All the same, the unending anxiety of not knowing what he would do next was too much. "Tell me what you're doing. Before you do it."

"I'm going to tie your legs to the chair, so that I can focus on giving you all of my attention without constantly correcting you. It's slowing us down." His tone was even, calming. Her nerves settled as he continued to stroke her hair. "Do you want me to touch you?"

Pulsing heat rushed between her legs. She clenched her thighs, as if she could hide it.

His chuckle sent another wave of need rushing through her. "I can smell you. You don't need to be shy, kitten. May we continue?"

Her thighs trembled as she obeyed. Cold air kissed her slick skin, and she shivered. Mia, the single-minded, driven scientist, was tied to a chair, spreading for him like an offering. And gods, she liked it. Anticipation burned low in her belly as she swallowed.

"You're so brave, kitten," he crooned as he wrapped silk rope around her calf, binding it to the chair leg. "But I expected that." His attention moved to her other side. "You've been on your own for so long. Won't it feel good to let someone else take control? To give you what you need?"

Coming from his lips, the idea was tantalizing. So much had happened. Hunters. Piper. Germund. It was like all at once the world went from predictable to a downright nightmare. "You won't abandon me? You promise to keep me safe?"

His hand trailed down the space between her breasts. "You're *mine*, kitten. In here. Out there. It doesn't matter. I protect what's mine. But I need you to trust me. Can you do that?"

Her heart hammered against her ribs. She was tied naked to a chair, with his hand on her belly, just inches from slipping inside her. *All you have to do is hand over the reins, and he'll do the rest.* "Yes."

His hand teased at her opening.

The chill of his touch only deepened her ache. She whimpered. Then he moved away. "No, don't stop."

His fingers circled at her center, parting her folds. "You're so perfect, kitten. Wet, and needy. Tell me how much you want me to touch you."

"Please, I want…" Her head tipped back as he blew cold air on her tender, wet, flesh. A shiver ran down her spine. He blew again, and it felt like the shadow of a kiss. Would he put his lips there? Bite her? *What the fuck, Mia?* Her stomach tightened in agonizing anticipation. A gentle brush of air against her aching center sent another pulse of pleasure through her. Gods, how was this turning her on? Was it the venom? Her own irrationality?

"Falling apart from nothing but air? Just wait until we really start to play." He dragged the back of his nails up her thigh. Inching closer to where she needed him. Then he pulled away. Again and again. Back and forth. Leaving her shivering.

She twisted in the restraints. "Isidore—

A sharp slap stung her thigh. "That's not my name in here."

"Please…my prince…" She moaned as he parted her folds, but didn't enter.

His thumb tapped her bundle of nerves. Drawing her ever closer to a cliff she could see, but couldn't reach. "Stay strong for me."

She trembled, the fire between her legs growing unbearable. Each brush of his fingers only stoked the flames higher. "Please…make it stop." Her voice cracked, barely more than a breath.

"Not yet, remember why we're here. You want me to protect you? To keep you safe? I need to restore my strength, and only you can do that for me."

A soft breath tickled her inner thigh. A tremor ran straight through her core. His body shifted, and the air cooled as he moved over her, his presence overwhelming. Vulnerability washed over her in waves, her desire for release becoming a test of endurance. Was this what she had wanted? To feel exposed and desperate? She was a doctoral candidate, for gods' sake. But it felt like nothing she'd experienced before.

Isidore knelt between her legs. He leaned closer, his breath tickling the skin of her stomach. She sucked in air as he kissed her, just above the naval. Gentle, teasing. Then he sank his teeth into her flesh. She writhed as another rush of venom set every one of her nerves on fire. A second later his tongue lapped at the weeping blood, soothing the throbbing left behind. His lips traced a languid path lower, dipping ever closer to the space where she ached. "We're almost done," he murmured, dragging his teeth along the curve of her hip. His fingers flexed against her thighs, pressing down with a possessive grip. "You're mine, kitten."

His fingers explored the deepest parts of her. Slow, deliberate. He pressed a sensitive spot hidden within. A choked cry escaped her lips as heat coiled in her belly, winding tighter with every stroke. Then his thumb moved. A sudden flick against her clit, sharp and electric, sent a violent shudder through her body.

Her hips jerked instinctively, lifting off the chair in search of deeper sensation that would bring sweet relief. The restraints were maddening. She slammed back down, breath ragged, muscles trembling as frustration tangled with pleasure.

"That's it. The more excited you are, the more I can absorb." He flicked his thumb, sending more rounds of agonizing bliss. "Just like that."

She panted for air as his hand slowed to a stop, still inside her. Everything felt sharp. The cool silk binding her.

Hard wood dug into her back. More of him was inside her. He shifted closer. With his other hand, he caressed and massaged her breast. Her body trembled, threatening to unravel. Then he was gone. She let out a broken whimper. He stroked the sensitive skin on her inner thigh. She writhed. The bindings dug into her. Fire felt like it was splitting her in two.

"So close…" His voice curled around her. "Just hold on a little longer, kitten. I'll take care of you. I'll give you exactly what you need."

His words washed over her like a promise. She wanted to resist, to keep the last shred of control. To prove, even to herself, that she could manage it all. But what was left to hold on to? What would she be proving? His grip flexed on her thigh, a quiet reassurance. This was real. This was hers to choose. And she chose him. "Please," she whispered, voice breaking. "I need you."

He slid his hand up, tantalizingly close. Then he pressed against her clit—hard, insistent. It sent a dazzling spark through her body, pleasure teetering on the edge of oblivion. Her breast ached as he tightened his grip. She seized, and white-hot pleasure ripped through her. Every muscle clenched, her back arching against the unyielding chair as a strangled cry tore from her throat. Raw, consuming.

Isidore's fingers kept moving. Relentless, dragging out tremors until she was nothing more than a shaking, gasping pile of nerves. Her skin burned with gold fire. The bindings dug into her wrists and ankles, anchoring her as wave after wave crashed through her.

"Isidore," she moaned before she could stop herself. Her mind was lost in his divine torment, incapable of forming sentences. A whimper escaped her lips as he withdrew his fingers, leaving her bereft. She'd been so close.

His free hand traced indistinct patterns down her stomach, then he pushed back inside. This time, there was no slow, teasing pressure or coaxing. It was strong. Possessive. Heat tore through her. She writhed, bucking against the restraints, chasing something she couldn't reach. He had her helpless, desperate, trembling on the edge. And still, he held her there, unrelenting.

His hand pressed down harder. Each breath was more erratic than the last. There was no escape from the spiraling sensation that consumed her. Each thrust of his fingers drove her, stripping her bare. Thoughts fragmented. His grip tightened as he pushed her further. She tensed, every muscle tightening as the sensation built higher, sharper, intolerable. Everything screamed for release. And when he finally, *finally* pushed her over the edge, there was a moment of weightlessness. Then pure, consuming pleasure ripped through her, stripping her down to raw sensation.

Chapter Twelve

sidore felt his kitten's energy humming beneath his fingertips as she writhed for him. He licked his lips, hovering just inches from her face as he knelt between her legs. Her fast, desperate breaths were a warm breeze on his cheek. The heat of her arousal ensnared him. The hunger was insatiable. It thrummed in the space between them, clawing at his insides, making every breath a struggle.

"You're mine," he whispered.

"Please," she breathed.

Gods, she was so close to her peak. Her body shivered beneath him, thighs trembling. He basked in her surrender. The sensual energy he'd nurtured to maturity was ripe for his picking.

He inhaled.

The violent thrill of her arousal flooded him, burning through every nerve like wildfire. He groaned, his body jerking as raw need crashed over him. Her sexual energy was everything he'd ever dreamed. It filled parts of him he hadn't known were empty. Every fiber of his being ignited into a symphony of renewal.

The demon unhinged its jaw, gulping her in. He stiffened, and his eyes fluttered closed as the sensation filled him. His cock pulsed. He was on fire. Standing, he stripped off his shirt, then shoved his too-tight jeans down and kicked them aside. He stopped short of taking off his boxers, a thread of reason reminded him he'd promised no penetration.

Her lips parted, a soundless breath escaping. He couldn't help the grin that pulled at his lips. *I can feel you, kitten.*

He straddled her sprawled legs. His weight sank down on her as his hips rolled forward—grinding against that soft, inviting heat between her thighs. She sagged against him, finally giving in to his control. A deep, rattling hiss escaped him as her soft breasts pressed into his chest. He rocked against her. Slow, deliberate, forcing his kitten to feel every inch of him.

The demon grew larger, and larger as he felt every emotion he'd forced on her while he'd brought her to the edge again, and again. Desperation. Anticipation. And gods, her arousal. The world felt like it was falling away until it was just them. Her body, her essence, everything she was now belonged to him.

He laid a claiming kiss on her lips. She moaned. He swallowed it. His feast. She was trembling beneath him, soft and pliant. Her breathing turned shallower, until she was gasping for air, drowning.

Pleasure was all he knew. Breathless, panting, he pressed

deeper against skin as cool as his own. Somewhere, deep in the haze, something shifted. The taste of her energy was less vibrant. Less alive. The weight beneath him changed. His demon ignored it, grinding harder, drinking deeper. More. He needed—

"Obsidian."

The word drifted through the thick haze of pleasure, but he was too caught up in the intoxicating rush of energy flooding his veins to process it.

She whimpered.

A ripple of cold pierced the consuming heat. He ignored it. More. He needed more.

She went limp beneath him.

The high shattered into a thousand jagged shards as reality slammed into him. Guilt and horror surged to the forefront as he finally took her in. Ashen. Cold. Limp. The demon hissed in his mind, writhing against his grip. It wasn't done. Would never be done. It bit at him, sibilating for more, its hunger a living thing, coiling and constricting around his gut. He thrust his mind past it, shoving through the suffocating urge, and the world sharpened around him.

"Mia?" He cupped her cheek, expecting fire, but her skin was ice. "Shit!"

His vision tunneled. The room tilted. His hands, slick with her sweat, shook uncontrollably as he fumbled at the knots. Too slow. *Gods, move.* His pulse thundered in his ears, drowning out her shallow breaths. *Breathe, fucking breathe.* Normally, there would be someone else to check the prey, clean them, handle the aftermath. But there was no attendant. No ritual. Just him. He cursed under his breath, frustration and panic coiling in his gut as he got the last restraint free and ripped the blindfold away. Crushing her against his chest, he bolted for the bathroom.

Gently, he propped her up against the wall as he drew a bath. *She's fine,* he coached himself. *It's just shock. Get her washed and into something warm. You've had this happen before.*

But it had never happened to someone he loved. That thought made his blood turn to ice. In his obsession-addled mind, he hadn't considered what the consequences would be of taking in the energy of another chaos being with alluring magic. Let alone one as powerful as her. Steam billowed in the small space as the water filled the tub.

Mia moaned.

He whipped his head around and crawled toward her, taking her hand in his. "Mia, it's over. You're okay."

Her eyes fluttered opened. She took a panicked inhale and looked wildly around the room.

"Shh, Princess. You're safe. Just relax and let me take care of you. You were incredible."

"Are you…" She eyed him warily.

"It's me in control."

She sagged with relief. "Did I do it right? What you needed?"

His throat locked. How could she ask that? How could she look at him like he hadn't just—his chest felt like it was being pulverized. She didn't know. Didn't even realize how close she had come to never waking up. Feeding wasn't supposed to be sexual. The ritual was meant to honor restraint. But tonight, it hadn't been a ritual. It had been a devouring. The demon hissed, satisfied. He wanted to rip it out with his bare hands. "Yeah," he forced out. She had done everything right. *He* was the one who had failed. "I'll make sure nothing happens to you. How are you feeling?"

"Sore…tired…" She took a shaky breath. "Cold."

"The bath will help." He pivoted back to the tub. It was nearly full, and he turned off the faucet. Steeling himself, he gathered her in his arms and slowly lowered her into the steaming waters.

She sighed and leaned back against the side.

"Mia, I don't know what your kind needs after something like this. You mentioned hot springs so…"

"This is perfect." Her voice was faint. "Warmth helps us heal faster."

"Can I wash you?"

Mia's golden eyes lifted and her brow furrowed. "Why?"

"Because it's my responsibility to take care of you. What we did in there…It was intense. Please, let me? I can wash your hair too."

She sighed, sinking into the water. "Mm…that would be nice."

He let out a breath. *She's okay.* He repeated it over and over, willing it to be true. His hands shook as he reached for the soap and lathered a washcloth. He braced her back as he began. Her head rolled so it was resting on his chest, and he couldn't help but admire her sensual curves as he made long strokes down her arms. Torso. A pressure built between his legs. Fuck, she was beautiful. He gave himself a shake and focused. When he finished her body and hair, he picked her up out of the bath and sat her down on the chaise he'd had her kneel on. The room still smelled of her arousal.

"Isi…"

The sound of the childhood nickname on her lips was something he'd never get enough of. "Yeah?"

"Can we sleep in my room?"

A thrill ran through him. She'd said *they* could sleep in her room. The relief that crashed over him almost drew a sob from his lips. He stuffed it down. There was only her tonight. "Yeah, anything you need, Princess. Just say it and I'll make it happen."

He carried her to the bed in the guest room and lay down next to her. She was warm in his arms now, her breathing soft and even, her body curled against him like she belonged there. But the weight in his chest only grew heavier with each passing second.

He wasn't supposed to lose control like that. Not with anyone, but especially not with the woman he had fallen in love with. He pressed a lingering kiss to her hair, swallowing against the tightness in his throat. She trusted him. And tonight, that trust was misplaced. Feeding wasn't supposed to be something you got sexual gratification out of. It was a sacred practice passed down through the ages as a reminder that they were living in more civilized times. He finally understood why more lamiae didn't take other chaos beings for life partners very often. It was too complicated.

Could he give up Mia? Never taste her sweet essence again? His stomach tied itself into knots. That was a bleak thought. She was perfect. Smart, brave, powerful. Good. Heat gathered in his groin as he focused on her soft, warm flesh against his. He hadn't known her long, but if her possessive attitude toward Piper was anything to go on, he doubted she'd be okay with him performing the ritual on other people. Would she offer herself to him every month? Excitement fluttered, commingling with guilt. He imagined what it would be like to feel this full all the time. Not just his hunger. She filled his mind, body, and spirit. If they ever did this again—and he really hoped they would—they needed safety checks. A lot of them. For her. For him. A full contract that defined the perimeters of the ritual and their relationship. But not like the ones his cabal used for prey kept in their households. Something that honored her divinity.

His demon had been caught off guard by her refusal to comply. It was used to patrons who craved submission. Mia was different. She had given him everything tonight, but out of trust instead of obedience. And he had nearly broken it. His demon wasn't sorry. It had gotten what it wanted. What it would always want. If she let him stay he would need an entirely new way of thinking about the feeding ritual. He would need to be better.

Chapter Thirteen

Mia woke to find herself lying next to a soothing cold. She turned on her side and snuggled closer, wrapping her arms around that comforting sensation. Then her eyes snapped open and she found herself staring into Isidore's dazzling green gaze. Her lips parted in a silent intake of breath. A flush came to her cheeks as she remembered what they'd done. What he'd done. What she'd *let* him do.

He stroked her hair. "Good afternoon, Princess."

"What?"

"It's two in the afternoon."

She blinked. That couldn't be right. She never slept that late, there wasn't any time.

"I ordered you something to eat. It's waiting for you downstairs." He caressed her cheek with his fingertips. "Are you okay?"

"I'm sore…" She didn't want to be more specific. The area that was sore wasn't one she wanted to discuss, even if he'd already seen everything there was to see down there. *And touch.*

"I have ibuprofen here for you. Do you want to soak in the bath again? I have some Epsom salt."

"I'll take the medicine. But we need to figure out how to save Piper."

He took in a slow breath and let it out. "They're more interested in you than Piper. She's just Jayce's tool for his career."

Agitation pushed all thoughts of her discomfort away. "Piper is not a tool!"

"Okay, shh…" He continued to stroke her hair, then her shoulder.

It soothed her, but she couldn't shake her unease. She hadn't sought out physical intimacy in years. Once, she'd tried dating, but her magic had made him too clingy, too possessive. When he tried to force himself on her, she ended it. But Isidore wasn't forcing her into anything. She had been the one to offer herself, and he'd rebuffed her. Twice. Her body relaxed and a low, contented purr rumbled in her chest as she sank deeper into his embrace.

"I'm sorry. I'll be more respectful of your charge."

"Good."

He chuckled softly. "We'll get her back. I sent a message to Germund to let him know what happened."

"I don't like him."

"You should more than not like him. He's one of the most dangerous chaos beings I know." His voice lowered, enunciating each word more slowly than the last. "Don't ever trust a word he says."

She shivered and clung more tightly to his shirt. "Why are you working with him?"

"Because…he's the most dangerous being I know. You don't say no to the heir of the Storm Feathers unless you've got a death wish—or an army to back you up."

"Did you call for backup?"

Seconds ticked by as she waited for his response. "I can't."

"Why?"

"Because my father will probably order me to abandon you, and I'll have to disobey. Then we're going to have a bigger problem."

"What happens if you disobey?"

He let out a quiet hiss. "I told you demons don't like to be told no. Let's leave it there."

Despite the warmth of the blankets, she shivered. His arms wrapped around her, drawing her into his chest. He pressed a lingering kiss to her hair.

"You're mine, Princess. Now more than ever. No one touches you if there's something I can do about it."

Her lips parted, then closed. Is that what she wanted? To be possessed? *To belong,* something inside her whispered. Her heart ached as she wondered what it might be like to belong to someone like that.

A phone buzzed. Isidore grumbled and let go of her so he could reach to the nightstand and look at the screen. "Fuck…Germund is coming here. Again."

Her chest tightened. "What do we do?"

"Get dressed, take medicine, and eat. You're shaking, and you need to rehydrate before you pass out on me."

Her limbs felt like lead. The moment she got up, her vision blurred at the edges, her legs trembling under her weight. A strong arm wrapped around her waist.

"Easy," Isidore murmured, steadying her. "You okay?"

She took a slow breath, willing her body to cooperate. "Yeah…just need a second." But even as she pulled away, her legs wouldn't stop shaking as she slowly made her way to the dresser where he'd laid out clothes for her. Jeans, a basic T-shirt, her college hoodie. Underwear. She felt his watchful gaze on her back as she got dressed. *He's just making sure you don't fall onto the dresser,* she chastised herself.

The bed creaked and then clothes rustled as he pulled on his shirt and jeans. He rested his hand at the small of her back as he led her to the stairs, then moved in front of her in case she fell. Mia couldn't decide if she found this endearing, or irritating. She wasn't a helpless damsel in distress. *But aren't you?* The thought stoked her frustration. She was floundering in this world she'd been unwillingly thrust into. A world her people had abandoned her in with no guidance.

When they reached the ground floor, Isidore led her to the dining room table. Falafel, hummus, grilled chicken gyro, stuffed grape leaves, and a Greek salad covered half of the already large table. The aroma of za'atar, cumin, coriander, and turmeric all tingled in her nose. "Isi…What?"

"I didn't know what you'd like," he said as he slid into a seat across from her.

Her stomach growled loudly, but still she didn't move. No one had ever taken care of her like this. Given her gifts, sure. People were always doting favors on her, trying to get more of her attention because they craved her alluring magic. But no one actually *saw* her.

Isidore tapped his thumb on the table. "Do you not like Greek food?"

She flushed and grabbed a falafel, biting into the crisp, golden shell before she had to voice her thoughts. The first rush of flavors made her eyes flutter. Warm cumin, nutty tahini, a hint of lemon. A groan slipped past her lips before she could stop it.

"So you do like Greek food. Excellent. You'll be eating a lot of it, since that's all I know how to make."

"Why did you learn to cook if you don't usually eat…human food?" She hid her verbal stumble by taking a stuffed grape leaf.

The coy smile on his lips spread. "You can't always avoid humans. Plus, it tastes good."

"I don't understand how your family functions. It sounds almost like a mafia thing, but weirder."

"Kinkier is the word you want."

She shot an annoyed glare at him. "Are you making fun of me?"

His expression sobered and he straightened. "Gods, no. You gave me something incredible, I'd never make fun of you for that. I'm making fun of my family."

Her muscles relaxed. "Sorry…I'm just…" She couldn't think of what to say and focused on eating.

"You don't have to be embarrassed. What happened last night stays between us."

She held the falafel in a grip that almost had the insides spilling out. "Swear it?"

"On my life."

She studied his face. No smirk, no teasing lilt. No gritty earthy taste of a lie. Just conviction. She let out a breath of relief. "Thanks."

He relaxed and took a sip of his coffee. "When Germund gets here, please try and talk as little as possible? I don't want him to know more about you than he already does."

"Why?"

His finger traced the etched designs on the outside of his mug. "You're not just an individual to him, Mia. You're a resource. A bargaining chip. The kind of discovery that reshapes power structures."

The hair on the back of her neck stood on end. "What?"

"He likes power. You get that by knowing things others don't, especially if that thing is a group of divine nishutu the world thought was dead. There are a lot of people who would pay fistfuls of money for that kind of information. The Storm Feathers have survived this long because they methodically took out stronger nishutu over the centuries. It's why they're the most powerful group in Canada, plus they've got a stronghold in New England. You already told him you're from his territory. That will make him even more interested, since you're obviously not from Baffin Island."

"I never thought of it like that." That was the sort of thing she ought to know. She felt like a child again as it hit her that telling Isidore the truth about her nature had been a potentially lethal mistake. The kind of mistake that could kick off a genocide—and it would be all her fault. Her grip on her falafel slipped as she struggled to breathe through the mounting pressure crushing her lungs."

Hey…" Isidore reached across the table and took her hand in his. "I told you that I would protect you. That includes protecting you from Germund, and people like him. I would rather be torn to shreds by the beasts of kur than betray you or your people."

She nodded, holding back the tears that were threatening to flow. It was all too much. Her hand slid out from his and she wrapped her arms around herself.

Isidore was up and kneeling beside her in the blink of an eye. He put his finger to her chin and gently moved her head so she was forced to look at him. "Talk to me. What's wrong?"

"I feel…stupid…exposed…"

"Shh…" He wrapped his arms around her in a tight embrace. "You're not stupid. And anytime you start feeling like this, remember that you could probably kill me without breaking a sweat."

She laughed weakly. "What?"

He leaned back just enough to hold her gaze. "Princess, you're a step below a goddess. You might not have taken on your full form yet, but I can feel it simmering in there, waiting to bust out of that cage it was in. With that massive energy boost you gave me last night, I can hold my own against Germund. But you? You'll be so beautiful when you take your form."

"You don't even know what it would look like."

"I don't have to. It's you. You're always beautiful."

Affection swelled in her chest. "Thanks."

A pounding knock from the front door made them jump. Isidore was on his feet and striding out of sight. A moment later, Germund came storming in.

"You didn't get *anything*? I swear, you're the most useless *fucking* lamia I've ever worked with!"

Isidore walked slowly behind him. His eyes were dark, and magic sizzled just under the surface of his skin. "Hello to you too."

Mia stared wide-eyed at the anzu. For a moment, words eluded her. Then she realized he'd insulted her lamia. "He's not incompetent! He was shot!"

Germund's brows knit together as his gaze landed heavily on Isidore. "You look fine."

"I healed." His hands opened and closed into fists at his sides. "If you would take a beat, we could strategize instead of yell."

"You healed?" Germund asked incredulously. His eyes drifted back to Mia, and a knowing smile crept across his face that didn't meet his eyes. "I would think you'd be more cautious about feeding on another nishutu. Did he tell you, girl, that he nearly killed the last one?"

Isidore's aura was a storm about to break. "Knock it off!"

Germund let out a cold bark of a laugh. "You weren't that powerful the other day. I guess you really did make a night of it."

Mia wanted the earth to open up and swallow her. "Strategy! How do we save Piper?"

"You would only care about your precious muse." Germund crossed his arms over his chest. "We have to offer a trade. A fake one. Mia for the muse—"

"Fuck no!" Isidore hissed.

"A *fake* one," Germund repeated in a warning tone. "We tie her up, bring her to the rendezvous site, and then take out their side."

Mia's heart pounded in her chest. This would be the third time in as many days she'd found herself restrained. All of them in wildly different contexts, and only one she secretly enjoyed.

"Too risky," Isidore said through clenched teeth.

"Then we wait, and those hunters will relentlessly hound her, while she hovers in their orbit because she refuses to abandon the muse."

His cold calculation made her shudder. He wasn't wrong. Piper was her charge—she would never abandon her. The hunters knew that now that she'd tried to rescue her. Mia's breath came in sharp, shallow gasps. Her wrists ached from the memory of zip ties digging into her. Could she do this? Let herself be tied up again? Exposed? Vulnerable? Her pulse pounded in her ears. But Piper needed her. "I'll do it," she whispered. "If Isidore is there the entire time." Trusting someone she'd just met was insane. But she'd already trusted him, several times, and he hadn't let her down. Every word from his lips so far had been sincere.

Isidore's eyes narrowed as if he were running through

scenarios in his head. He swallowed. "Mia stays with me the entire time. You don't lay a finger on her."

"Possessive," Germund jibed. "Fine. I'm assuming you have something here we can use. Should probably gag her too; she's a little too chatty for a captive."

Isidore looked like he wanted to rip Germund's face off. "We're not doing anything until we have to."

"Great, glad you agree. I've already made the arrangements. We're leaving now."

Chapter Fourteen

From the moment Isidore heard the pounding on the door, he knew the illusion of sanctuary would come crumbling down on his head. But he hadn't been prepared for Germund to pivot on a dime and suggest using Mia as bait. He was all too aware that the anzu was making a grab for power to control the narrative. His knee-jerk reaction was to slam down the idea and tell the bastard to get the fuck out. Which would play right into Germund's hands and give him an excuse to escalate tensions. What Isidore needed was time to think. "We're not going anywhere until I say so."

A muscle in Germund's brow twitched. "You lost the privilege of being in control when you messed up with the muse."

Mia wrapped her arms around her middle as she took a half step back.

Isidore's hand shot out and wrapped around her wrist. "Come here…" He gently tugged until she unfurled, then caught her weight as she tipped forward. His attention snapped up to Germund. "Sit in the living room and don't move."

The only reply was a low grumble, but Isidore ignored it. He led Mia into the kitchen. Shadows came to his call, hugging them tightly and blanketing them in silence so his unwanted houseguest couldn't overhear.

"Mia...Are you sure you want to do this?"

Her head jerked up and gold fire flared in her eyes. "I have to!"

He felt like he was about to be dragged under a raging current by a monster he didn't want to name. "You don't. We can find another way—"

"Like what?"

His throat tightened. Wisps of potential options flew past him like leaves in the wind. Calling his family wasn't an option. His father would order him to do nothing, Dimitra might be on board, but he didn't trust her to not undermine Mia's safety for some kind of power play he couldn't guess at. All of his friends were too far flung for a last-minute summons. He rubbed a hand down his face. "He has an angle," he choked out. "I don't know what it is." The admission felt like he was exposing himself to be slaughtered. This wasn't how he worked. He was supposed to be in control, to see the moves on the board before his opponent made them. But all he saw was Mia, with her shining golden essence that would be a beacon to every shady faction within five hundred miles if it got out that she wasn't under anyone's protection. *She's under yours,* he reminded himself.

"I *have* to do this." She took his hand in hers as her voice dropped in pitch. It rumbled deep in her throat, rattling his bones. "I know you don't understand, and it's hard to explain because what little I know of my own magic comes from half-remembered stories. But my people cut themselves off because we literally can't help ourselves from intervening when we think someone is in danger. Piper is mine to protect until she doesn't need me anymore."

Each breath felt like effort as the weight on his chest grew unbearable. Mia dissolved, replaced by a thin man with yellow eyes. Basim had thrown himself headfirst into danger because his divine essence couldn't tolerate injustice.

He slammed his eyes shut on the sukkalu, but it didn't block out the smell of his blood. Earthen, and briny. Like the wetlands along the coast. He blinked open his eyes and saw Mia once more. If he expected her to accept all of him, dark snake demon and all, then he needed to accept her as the divine creature she was. Duty bound to defend those she deemed worthy. He swallowed and cupped her cheek. It was too easy to see her lying dead on the ground at his feet. That protective instinct had gotten Basim killed, and it could kill her too if she didn't have help. He licked his dry lips. If he wanted to protect Mia then it meant protecting her charge.

"Okay, Princess," he rasped.

She leaned closer. "I'm not the sukkalu—nothing that happens today will be your fault."

Her scent washed over him and he pulled her flush against his chest. She was warm, and perfect in his arms.

He pressed a lingering kiss against her hair. In his soul he knew the divine essence in her believed those words. Thought that it could rely on itself like it always had to get through life. But like his demon, her divinity didn't consider real-world implications. Their chaos spirits had been forged at a time when myths were real and divine power was respected. Now they were just more things for the monsters to covet and own. He lifted her chin and searched her golden eyes without even knowing what he was looking for. Then her lips were against his. Soft, and silken. Warm and tender. Magic sizzled between them as her fire and his shadows mixed. He brushed his tongue against her bottom lip. She parted for him and he plundered deeper. He took a sharp intake of breath. His hand slid down her shoulder and he cupped her sculpted breast. Life pulsed under his lips as he kissed her jawline. Last night had been about nothing but feeding the worst parts of himself. This was for him. To remind himself that a lamassu wanted him despite all of the horrible things he'd done.

"I won't let anything happen to you," he whispered in her ear. "When this is over, you, me, and Piper are coming back here."

She pulled away to study him. "What?"

He caressed her cheek with his thumb. "You can't survive without protection. I don't just mean right now, or today. Germund knows about you, and we can't walk that back. I'm offering you and your charge the protection I can provide as a prince of the House of Crimson Fang." His voice caught and he swallowed. "It's not as good as if my sister—"

"I accept." Her eyes widened as if her own words shocked her.

Isidore's heart thudded, then he smiled. "Then promise me that you'll do everything I tell you today? So all three of us come home safely?"

Her eyes glistened as she nodded. The air sparked with magic as she pulled him into another kiss. He held her until the shadows wavered. Lightning flickered and Germund's muffled voice sounded through the shadows.

"Are you two done?"

Reluctantly, Isidore let her go. He gave himself a shake as he let his demon rise back to the surface. The muscles in his face tensed as he took up a well-practiced mask. When the shadow shield fell, he faced Germund as the prince of the Crimson Fangs. "Now we can leave. We're taking my car, and I'm driving."

Germund clenched his teeth but said nothing as he spun on his heel and marched toward the door.

Isidore turned to face Mia and held out a hand. "Come on…You're sitting in the front with me."

~

By the time they arrived at a parking lot Isidore had scouted out, his hands ached from the death grip he had on the steering wheel. He'd kept half an eye on Germund in the review mirror, and was not pleased when he caught the bastard staring at Mia five too many times. It just reinforced what he already knew. Mia was, without a doubt, his newest obsession. Which was not the kind of thing he wanted to be fully aware of right before tying her up and leaving her more vulnerable than she already was. He glanced sideways at her. She was pale, and her hands shook in her lap. The fire of her divine essence had faded, leaving behind very human fear. He lingered in the car as Germund slammed his door shut.

"Mia." He tried to keep his voice low, but she jumped and stared at him through wide eyes. "I think Germund might try to lure you away by threatening Piper. It's incredibly important that you stay levelheaded."

"Why would he do that?"

This is new for her, he reminded himself as frustration bubbled up. Mia had spent her whole life running, but she didn't know what it meant to be hunted. Not yet. Her instinct to protect would be her greatest weakness. It made her predictable. Vulnerable. And if Germund had figured that out? Then they were already at a disadvantage. "Because he's pieced enough together that you're tied to her. If he goes for her, I want you to stay with me until the human threat is gone. *Then* we go after Germund together. You can overpower him, but he's better trained. I'm more controlled and experienced, but he's stronger than me. If we work together, then we can take him down."

She gave a small nod. "Okay."

He hesitated for one more breath, trying to stretch this moment out for as long as possible. If he stayed calm and in control, then he could get her out of this in one piece. "Let's go."

Chapter Fifteen

Mia shoved her hands into the pockets of her hoodie as Isidore walked at her side. The forest was alive with noises. Every sound felt heightened. Sticks cracked. A squirrel jumped through the canopy of leaves. There was a deer in the distance, eating off a shrub. All the while, Mia could feel Piper's nerves growing stronger as they continued along the path. Germund was a few feet ahead of them, walking as if this were nothing but a leisurely stroll. Her stomach twisted as Isidore's warning came back to her. *You knew marking Piper put you at risk,* she chastised herself. But she hadn't fully realized everything she'd put at stake. Her one mission was supposed to be to stay anonymous so that she could fulfill her sacred responsibility as the maru hiptu. And what had she done? Thrown it all away because her divine side had gotten the better of her. Anger mixed with helplessness. None of this would have happened if Gordon had prepared her. Or if her roommate hadn't stolen her stupid amulet. If she hadn't gone out the day she met Piper. She bit her lip and ducked her head so no one could see the tears gathering in her eyes. Isidore was already struggling with this, he didn't need to watch her break down. Germund would only see it as yet another vulnerability to exploit. *Pathetic,* she thought viciously.

Isidore pulled her to a stop, and gently forced her head up. "Take a breath," he whispered. "You're panicking."

She jerked out of his hold and wrapped her arms around herself. For a moment all she could think about was how much she wanted to go back to the island, to her mother. That was the last time she had felt safe.

"Is there a problem?" Germund's voice was cold, almost jeering.

"Back off!" Isidore snapped. "We'll catch up."

"Whatever." The anzu turned and continued down the path.

Mia squeezed her eyes shut as a war broke out in her soul. Fiery gold against suffocating fear. Both used up all the oxygen, leaving her gasping. A pair of arms threaded around her, and she was pulled into Isidore's embrace. The reassuring pressure shocked her lungs back into movement. Her chest expanded, pressing against his. Slowly, she returned the embrace. The racing thoughts calmed, until rational thought returned. "You swear we go home after this?"

"Yes, and not just to that lifeless shell of a house. We'll find a new one that has more character."

She laughed hollowly and pressed her forehead against

his shoulder. "Okay. I'm sorry, I'm the one who insisted on doing this, and I'm—"

"Don't." He pulled away and kissed her gently. "I was scared on my first op too."

"What's an op?"

The corner of his mouth twitched in the shadow of a smile. "Operation. Just do what we said."

A rustling sounded as they broke apart, and Germund came back into view. "They're just over the ridge. Might want to get our *trade* ready."

Isidore's nostrils flared, but he pulled a pair of zip ties out of his pocket. "You'll be able to break out of these easily if you need to." His voice was steady, calm. But she could see the tempest in his eyes. "Just tap into your divine self…"

The thought of using magic was unpleasant, but she kept that thought to herself. "Okay."

"I'll be right there. When shit goes down, take Piper and run."

"I'm not leaving you."

His lips pressed into a thin line. "Mia, you're exhausted. Don't take this on."

She wrapped her arms more tightly around herself, desperately trying to conceal her anxiety yet knowing she was failing miserably. "Okay."

He took her wrists, prying them away from her waist, then held them together as he secured the zip tie. "Remember that you're in control."

She didn't feel like it as he tightened the binds. He tied a knot in a length of silk rope. Probably one he'd used last night. Gently, he pushed the knotted ball in the center into her mouth and tied it in place. He took her arm in a firm grip and led her up the path behind Germund. It didn't take long for her to hear the footsteps of humans. She frowned. There were more than just Jayce and Sage. Four people were shifting and pacing through the undergrowth up ahead. She instinctively tried to warn Isidore of the danger, but her words were blocked.

Isidore raised a brow at her, but they came to the clearing too quickly. At the other end, Jayce and Sage flanked Piper. Mia's gaze zeroed in on her charge, trying to assess her physical condition. She was bound, gagged, and blindfolded. Hell for a Deaf woman. Her head was bent down, and her brown hair fell like a worn-out curtain over her face.

Jayce's eyes flicked between Mia and Isidore, his grip tightening on his gun. "You just let her walk?" His voice was sharp, incredulous. "Are you insane? She's a goddamn weapon."

Germund smirked, flashing pointed silver teeth. "Not to us. But to you?" He chuckled darkly. "You should've killed her when you had the chance."

Sage scowled. "One of you walks her over here, then we hand over the muse."

Isidore's grip tightened on her arm. Mia's legs shook as they started forward. She felt like she was walking in her own funeral procession.

Again.

They came to a halt. Tension crackled like lightning.

Then chaos magic erupted. Mia's head whipped to the side in time for a gust of wind to throw dust into her face. She blinked rapidly to clear her vision. A giant, winged, four-legged eagle streaked past in a flurry of dark gray feathers. Germund's talons were extended as he charged at Sage. Isidore threw Mia behind him as he launched himself forward. His body shifted and writhed in midair as shining onyx scales replaced skin. The bottom half of his body became the shadowy form of a serpent's tail, and he let out a spitting hiss of rage.

Sage gave a shriek of fury as Germund slammed into her, talons raking her skin. Jayce was already moving. A gunshot cracked through the trees. He fired again, this time at Isidore. The lamia hissed, coiling to the side as the bullet missed and buried itself into a tree trunk.

Mia's heart raced. Two more humans were closing in. Jayce was reloading fast, his hands steady despite the chaos. Then Isidore struck and his teeth sank into Jayce's neck. Blood poured out in a sickening rush. Jayce let out a gurgled yell as Isidore dropped him, crimson dripping from his fangs. Mia's stomach turned. He lunged for another human.

Piper screamed.

Magic pumped through Mia at the sound of her charge's distress. Strength flooded her exhausted muscles, and she ripped apart the zip ties, then pulled off the gag. She sprinted toward Piper, who was trembling on the ground in terror. Sage's body was a ruin of shredded limbs on the blood-streaked earth. The metallic tang of her blood clung to the air, thick and suffocating. *Just get Piper*, Mia recited as she fell to her knees and frantically tried to work at the rope ties. Her fingers were shaking too much to get a grip. Another shriek ripped the air. Lightning struck the ground next to her, and Mia used her body to shield Piper from the shower of rock and dirt.

Talons tore through the muscles on her back, and searing white-hot pain shot along her shoulders. She barely had time to gasp before she was ripped off her feet and hurled like a rag doll. Her back slammed into a tree with a sickening crack. She struggled to breathe as she gasped and watched in horror as Germund partially changed back to a human form with wings. He seized Piper, then launched into the sky.

Fury ignited, pushing out the bone-deep exhaustion in a final surge of energy. Hot. Blazing. Seething. It roared through her veins like molten fire, burning away every fragile thread of restraint. Her skin rippled like liquid gold. *Stay with me.* Isidore's voice echoed in her memory, a distant whisper swallowed by the roaring fire. Her spine arched. Bones snapped. Clothes melted away. Wings burst from her back, unfolding with a deafening whoosh. Her fingers curled, claws slicing through the dirt as her hands became massive paws. A tail lashed behind her. She lunged forward, powerful and wild, as her wings flapped, sending dust and leaves swirling. Every thought in her mind was crowded out by her single, obsessed focus. Her weight lightened, then she was airborne, streaking through the canopy after her charge. *"You will not take her!"* Her roar split the air apart.

Germund looked over his shoulder and blanched.

Satisfaction twisted in her gut. *You can't outrun me,* she thought. His wings beat against the air, as he frantically searched for more speed. But she was faster. He dove for the ground. Her inner essence snarled as it sniffed out his dark aura. She was going to rip him limb from limb for daring to touch what she had marked for divine protection. Her body slammed into his, the impact sending shockwaves through her bones. Piper tore free, a blur of motion plummeting toward the trees. Mia dove. Thunder cracked, and the world was lit up by a flash of blue. Then pain. Burning through her like a brushfire. She screeched as she lost control and hurtled toward the ground. Branches bit at her skin as she fell, and her body was tossed in a disorienting spiral. Then she slammed into the hard ground with a bone-splintering crash.

A ragged breath tore from her throat and sharp pain knifed through her ribs. Dust and scattered leaves clung to her sweat-drenched fur. Germund landed with a thunderous crash, shifting midmotion. His body stretched, bones reforming as he took on his full chaos form. He was massive. Covered in feathers that shimmered with stormy blue magic. His maw split open his face as he displayed the rows of vicious, silver fangs. Then he lunged. Slashing, clawing. She roared in fury and lashed out with primal rage. A part of her knew she was outmatched. She was worn out from the feeding ritual, exhausted from days of life-and-death ordeals. But she didn't care. The earth was her canvas and his blood her paint. She would see this monster eviscerated, even if it was the last thing she ever did.

Chapter Sixteen

sidore's lungs burned as he whipped through the forest, his serpentine form moving with deadly speed as he cut through the shadows. Anger burned in his veins. He'd told her not to take off. Warned her that Germund wanted her. He sniffed the air, following the unmistakable scent of Mia's divine energy. All his frustration dissolved as the moment she transformed flashed in his mind. Mia was fire given form. A massive lioness, her fur shifting through a breathtaking spectrum of earth reds, oranges, and molten gold, like the sky at the moment of creation. Every inch of her rippled with untamed power. Her chest was broad, muscular. Magnificent wings stretched out, showing off their plumage, and her hair. Gods. Her hair was wild, like the mane of a lion. Auburn, with the same unsettling earthen colors. A pair of elongated ears poked through the mane. Slender. Almost delicate. But it was her eyes that sent chills to his core. Golden fire, with catlike slitted pupils. Matching golden flames wrapped around her like vines.

Lightning burst ahead of him. His ears rang when a roar sent a shockwave through the forest. He pushed himself to the limit as he raced forward, knowing that Mia had to be at the end of her strength. There was the sickening crunch of a large body slamming into the ground. As he darted through the last of the shrubs, he wound to a halt.

Mia pounced, striking like a beast hunting prey. Germund dove out of the way too slowly. Her claws hooked into his flesh, tearing through feather and skin with ruthless efficiency. He screeched and twisted, but Mia's massive paws slammed him back down, her fangs snapping inches from his throat. The anzu pivoted and struck back. His talons raked her sides.

Mia was all feral instinct. Germund, a cold tactician. Isidore saw the plan immediately. Hold out. Let her burn through her reserves. Then strike when she had nothing left. Isidore focused on Mia. Her magic had dimmed. Each strike became less precise. Slower. Weaker. His heart was in his throat. Stepping between them would be suicide. *That's Mia, your princess.* He hissed and shot forward. His magic surged as he called on the shadows. They converged around Germund, plunging him into darkness. Mia startled back, her head whipping around until she spotted him. Her ears flicked in recognition, but her movements were sluggish, and her stance was uneven. He could feel her magic dimming like a flame on the verge of snuffing out.

A sick, ice-cold panic settled in his stomach. If she faltered, Germund would rip her apart. Isidore dove at their opponent a split second before her. His fangs dug into Germund's wing, dragging him to the ground as Mia aimed a blow. Germund wrenched his wing free with a snarl, twisting. Too late. Mia's claws raked across his side. He soared backward and slammed into the ground. Isidore was on him. Fangs sank deep as he pinned his prey down.

Germund screeched and writhed. Dark and gold blood splattered the ground. Mia made for a strike, but a blast of lightning knocked her off her paws. Isidore's grip on his opponent weakened, then Germund threw him off. He thrashed his wings in a desperate attempt to escape. Isidore dove, but Germund lifted off just in time, streaking toward the sky. Isidore hissed. Coiling and uncoiling in frustration. An eerie, unearthly whine set his teeth on edge. Then he saw Mia. She was sprawled on her side, massive paws twitching, her flank rising in ragged, shallow breaths. Blood seeped from jagged wounds, pooling beneath her in golden, shimmering puddles. He slithered toward her.

"Mia!" His hands were shaking. He stroked her feather-soft mane, cradling her closer as her golden blood trickled through his fingers. "You'll be okay." A lie. A pathetic, desperate lie. He could see the creeping stillness overtaking her. Her eyes were unfocused. The breath that left her parted lips was barely more than a whisper. A sheen of sweat clung to her fur, catching the faint light like a dusting of frost. Wild panic sank its iron claws into his chest. It was happening again. Mia faded, replaced by Basim lying unconscious on the ground as Germund yanked a knife out of the sukkalu's torso. The demon's insatiable hunger had left both Basim and Mia too weak to defend themselves against threats, condemning them both to death. "Princess, tell me what you need? What can help you?"

Her glassy eyes found his. Her lips parted as if to speak, but no words came out. A shudder wracked her body.

"Please, Mia…" He frantically tore through every conversation, every casual aside, every half-whispered secret she had let slip. A memory crashed into him. The first time they'd met, in a forest like this.

"If I'm hurt I can absorb life essence from others to heal."

He clutched her closer, his breathing erratic. "Mia, how do you absorb life essence?"

For half a breath her eyes focused, and her fur bristled. Her front paws twitched weakly against him, as if she were trying to push him away. "Don't…I have…to breathe…But not with you…" Her throaty rasp was barely audible.

"I don't understand what that means!" Isidore's voice cracked, the weight of his helplessness clawing at his throat. His hands trembled as he gripped her, as if sheer force of will could keep her tethered to him. Her eyelids drooped.

"No, you are not dying!" Not when it was his fault she'd been left like this. A sharp, suffocating pressure wrapped around his lungs, like a rope tightening around his throat. There had to be something. Anything.

Then it hit him.

He cupped her face and ran his thumb along the fine, velvety fur on her cheek. Then his lips pressed against hers. He exhaled, pouring his breath into her.

A soft, warm glow pulsed beneath his fingers. Her body

jerked violently. She gasped—a ragged, desperate sound. Her lips parted, and this time, she didn't just take his breath. She siphoned something deeper. A sharp, visceral pull wrenched through his chest as the edges of his essence blurred. His lungs seized. A sudden weight crushed his ribs. The pull was slow, and deep. Like an ocean tide dragging him under. Relentless, inescapable.

Her soft exhale was warm, and he breathed in her sweet golden essence. It expanded into a silken mist that spread through his lungs, then into his veins. His heart pumped wildly, sending that light pulsing through him. It collided violently with the icy shadows of his soul, sending out a thunderclap that threatened to rip him apart.

Raw instinct screamed at him to retreat. His muscles bunched, his hands twitched—every nerve in his body clamored at him to escape the chains he felt forming. *No, I will not live without her!*

She drew in more. He shook as he fought against his impulses. Golden vines sprouted from the mist inside him. They twisted and wound around his insides. Pain ripped through his chest as thorns dug into his demonic core. Something snapped, and the bindings tightened until he thought he'd suffocate.

A guttural sound rumbled from deep within her chest. Then came a crack, and the grotesque, stomach-churning sound of bones snapping, shifting, realigning in a violent ballet. Her body convulsed against him, sinew and muscle twisting beneath his fingertips. She collapsed. Isidore caught her, cradling her close. His own breath came in ragged gasps, his arms trembling as he held her limp, fragile body against him.

He held still, trembling and savoring the steady beat of her heart. Blood still oozed from her cuts, but they weren't as deep. He'd never seen healing magic like this. Never heard of one being taking the life force of another, instead of feeding on their emotions. But it didn't matter. She was alive. Breathing. Warm.

Slowly, the world came back into focus. The late-afternoon air, filled with the damp, earthen smell of spring, pressed around him. He couldn't stop trembling. Something foreign and intimate pulsed inside him like a heartbeat, out of sync with his erratic pulse. He stared down at Mia and caressed her pale face. A flicker of darkness caught his eye and he focused on the wavering aura around her. A wisp of hazy shadows clouded her usual essence. His breath caught. Unease crept up his spine, then along his arms, and an ache filled him. Dull at first, then it thrummed. It felt like he'd been thrashed by Germund's talons, not her. He clenched his teeth and breathed through the pain until it subsided into the background. His chest heaved as his mind caught up. It was her. He was feeling her pain, her injuries. The fluttering warm heartbeat was hers. His eyes snapped down to her and he watched as the flickering, shadowy aura receded.

His demon reared, baring its fangs. It coiled restlessly as it tried to avoid touching the golden vines that ensnared it into an unnatural cage. The bond shifted and tightened, like unseen chains going taut. His heart jolted as the thorns embedded into his bones. Then a lock clicked into place, and cold finality settled in his gut. He thrust the feeling aside and leaned down to press his lips against her forehead, absorbing the fevered heat coming from her skin. *She's alive.* He repeated the words in his mind. It was all that mattered. The rise and fall of her breaths. The beating of her heart. Everything else could wait for tomorrow.

Rustling leaves caught his attention. He whipped his head up and bared his fangs as magic flooded him, preparing to defend his lamassu at all costs. Then a brunette woman appeared. Her dark eyes were wide, framed in white. He could smell her terror from the other side of the clearing. Adjusting his hold, he motioned for Piper to move closer. She stayed frozen, her eyes darting between him and Mia.

"She's okay. You're okay. I'll get you both back home," he said. Then mentally kicked himself for trying to verbally explain something to a Deaf woman.

She inched closer, and her hands moved through air in signs he couldn't begin to decipher. The corners of her lips tipped down. Then she pointed at Mia and gave a thumbs-up, then a thumbs-down sign.

He gave a thumbs-up back, feeling faintly ridiculous. After everything they'd been through, he was left with replying by hand gestures that a child could understand. He pointed at her, then himself, then mimed turning a steering wheel. Not elegant, but it hopefully got the point across.

Her lips pursed as she concentrated. Then she gave a tiny nod.

He sighed in relief. "We're getting the *fuck* out of here."

Chapter Seventeen

Mia's awareness gradually returned. She was lying in a warm, feather-soft bed. The sheets were like silk caressing her tattered skin. Her muscles screamed in protest as she moved, and she whimpered in pain. A door burst open. Her breath hitched, heart slamming into her ribs as she jolted back. Before she could scream, Isidore was already at her side, cupping her face.

"Shh—hey, you're okay." He stroked back her flyaway hair. "Princess, breathe."

The panic ebbed, replaced by bone-deep exhaustion. Her body ached in a way it never had before. Not just soreness. It was something deeper, colder. "Gods…I feel…like death."

"You took a hit when you were fighting Germund."

Memory crashed into her. Lightning. Blood. Piper. She lurched forward. "Piper, where—"

"Shh, she's okay." He caught her by the shoulders, guiding her back down before she tore herself apart. "She's in the guest room, safe. I promise. It's been a couple of days."

"Days?"

"Yeah, you were pretty out of it."

Alarm pierced through her. "Gods! My grades!"

His mouth opened, then closed. He pinched his lips. "I let the university know that there was a medical emergency. I told them that you would need to move your flight back, for your field work in Ecuador. The new flight is the first week of June."

Her brows furrowed. "How…"

"I found your student ID, *Amelia Whittaker*." He gave a weak smile. "I'm assuming that isn't the name you were born with."

"No…"

"What was your birth name?"

She had already given him so many pieces of herself. He had seen her at her most vulnerable, at her most vicious. Everything in between. So why was it so hard to tell him her name?

A cold pulse rippled through her chest, disrupting her thoughts. There was a shadowy, foreign presence coiling around her, sliding under her skin like a snake. The bone-deep cold clashed violently with the golden fire of her divine self, sending a shudder up her spine. She gasped, her breath caught as horror seized her. "Isidore…How am I alive?"

He went still, then licked his lips. "I let you take my life essence."

His words hit like a stone plummeting into a puddle. Inside her, the shadowy mist twisted, rippled, then pulsed. Like a heartbeat, steady. Grounding, yet wrong. Her mother's voice whispered in her memory, warning her that the life-saving rite was sacred, irreversible, and binding. A sick realization had bile burning her throat. She would feel him forever. He would feel her. There would be no distance, no escape, and she had to tell him. "The Breath of Life…It's a sacred rite, something that should only be done in a time of great need," she recited carefully.

"You were dying." His voice had a low, warning tone. "I'd call that pretty great."

Her heart thudded once. Twice. "It's…" Her fingers twisted in the sheets. "The connection that's forged is unbreakable, and the two lives are dependent on each other."

Isidore didn't move. He just watched her, eyes sharp.

"I'm not…entirely sure of the process," she admitted. "I remember my mother saying something about how there's a trade of some kind? I think the giver, you in this case, can pass along energy at will…And I think I'm sealed as your guardian. It was something we were supposed to use in the Divine Wars. So we could team up with allies, since we were mostly meant as protectors of the righteous. There's some kind of synchronicity that's supposed to happen, but I don't remember all of the specifics."

Something flickered behind his gaze, but she couldn't read the expression.

"I can feel you," she continued. "Your emotions. Your presence. If you need me…I'll know. You won't be able to hide from me, no matter what." She didn't want to say the rest. Burdening him with the full weight of what they'd done was too much.

His chin tilted down. "Mia, finish your explanation."

The order hung in the air between them, then words tumbled out of her. "It's supposed to be used with divine nishutus."

"I'm the opposite of divine…"

Her voice wavered. "There was a story about a traitor lamassu who bound to a sehru…a demon…" She licked her lips as the story floated to the surface of memories she tried to keep buried. "Some of their bond worked like normal—the lamassu could always feel where the demon was. And the demon could heal the lamassu. But…the bond was messed up. Instead of being enhancing, they were coerced into their roles. The lamassu couldn't ignore it if the demon called to them, and the demon could feel every injury of the lamassu. Once, when the demon almost died, they nearly took the lamassu with them, because their demon nature grabbed onto their life essence. Like how a drowning person will cling to a rescuer and drown them both in panic."

A heartbeat passed. Then Isidore inhaled slowly. "If I die, I'll end up killing you with me?" Jagged lines of darkness warped the space around him.

She wrapped herself in a tight hug. That wasn't the part that had left her with nightmares for weeks after she'd first heard the story. She couldn't bring herself to answer his question and focused on getting the story out instead. "It scared them, so they tried to find a way to sever the bond. But they couldn't get rid of it no matter what they did…" She didn't want to finish, but his gaze was earnest and unblinking. "The demon couldn't take it anymore, feeling the lamassu all the time. It changed them." She swallowed hard, pulse hammering. "So the demon killed the lamassu."

Isidore was eerily still as his aura darkened, and the shadows around him quivered. Mia could barely draw air as paralyzing fear held her in place. No demon could tolerate this kind of connection, it went against everything in their nature. She knew what he had to be thinking. It was written in every taut muscle of his body. He looked like a predator about to strike. She felt as if claws of darkness were sinking into her, dragging her toward the grave she had been denied for seventeen years. He shifted as he reached for her, and she flinched back. His hands wrapped around her wrists, his grip like cold iron. The world faded as he locked her into his piercing emerald gaze. With a sharp tug, he pulled her to his chest and wrapped his arms around her. His breath was hot against her temple, his grip firm, unrelenting. "Never tell that story again," he murmured. "To anyone."

Mia trembled in his embrace, her breaths shallow. His words didn't make any sense. She pushed against his chest as she tried to get free. "Didn't you hear me? The bond drove them insane—"

He silenced her with a hard, possessive kiss. It knocked the breath from her lungs. Her fingers gathered his shirt into a fist.

When he pulled back, his eyes were blazing. "I don't regret it. Not for a second, ancient wars be damned. But you cannot breathe a word of this to a single soul. It's dangerous, mostly to you."

"It can hurt you too! The demon, he—"

His hand gripped her chin. "Listen to me." There was an edge to his voice that cut through the air like a blade. "What you just described," he continued slowly, "is a perfect storm of how to lure you into a trap. You're valuable and powerful. More powerful than me, which means I'm the easier target. So you don't ever tell anyone that your life is tied to mine, or that you have this pull toward me. And I won't tell anyone that I can feel your injuries." He paused. A muscle in his jaw spasmed. "There's people who would call our bond a weakness…" His fingertips caressed her cheek, his gaze searching hers. "Weaknesses in my world aren't tolerated."

"But…"

His green eyes flashed a warning, and the words died on her lips. "What's your real name? The one you were born with?"

No one had ever looked at her like that, as if he truly saw through her defensive layers to a part of her that she'd tried to bury. Why did he want to know the name of a dead girl? It had nothing to do with anything. But his tone made it clear he was demanding, not asking.

Swallowing hard, she whispered, "Mialat."

His expression remained steady, calm. "Mialat." He said her name slowly, like he was tasting it.

Hearing her name on his lips shattered the last of her defenses. Not a soul had spoken her name since the leader had pronounced her death.

"Mialat." His tone was soft. "I wasn't there to save you

when your people killed you. But I'm here now, and I would do that Breath of Life rite a thousand times if it meant keeping you alive. No one is taking you from me. Not the hunters. Not the gods. Not even death."

There was no taste of earth. No lie. His words pierced the last vestiges of her fear, sinking deep into the recesses of her soul. A tear spilled down her cheek. She had spent so long running and guarding herself against connection because she was so afraid that no one could ever truly see her through the magic. And yet, here he was. A demon, forged in darkness, offering her everything. Not because he was compelled by magic, but because he chose her. An ache started in her chest as she allowed herself to feel his devotion through the fledgling bond between them. And Inanna help her, because she hadn't just bound herself to a demon. She had fallen in love with him.

Epilogue

Days blurred into weeks. Mia's grades were in, and summer session had officially started—not that she was teaching, since she was spending the summer in Ecuador. She stood in front of a painting in a house she and Isidore had just closed on. It was situated at the edge of a gorgeous park, where she could easily enjoy a walk. The house was empty, save for this one piece of artwork he'd somehow managed to secure and hang. An enormous landscape painting of the aurora borealis stretched across a night sky, over a white arctic tundra. Mia brushed her fingertips along the protective glass. The colors swirled, alive with memory. Her chest tightened and a lump formed in her throat. Seventeen long years, but she was finally home. The cooling, shadowy mist that bound her soul to Isidore's billowed and swirled, wrapping her in its comforting embrace.

The house was perfect. It had been built in the 1800s, and while its original charm had been chipped away by

1970s and '80s aesthetics, Isidore had already hired contractors to start restoring it. There was even space on the top floor for Piper. She purred at the thought of her charge. The young woman was still dazed, but Isidore had promised to keep her safe. Mia had been distressed to learn that there was a thriving muse trade. They were coveted for the same reasons Jayce had wanted her—muses were creative batteries that never ran out. Everyone from artists to people like Germund wanted one. Mia gave herself a shake to settle her nerves. It wasn't all her responsibility, though she had a niggling of unease that she'd inadvertently forced Isidore to extend his umbrella of protection to Piper.

A low vibration started between her legs and her breath caught. A blush crept up her cheeks. "Isidore!"

A dark, sultry chuckle echoed around the room as he slunk out of a shadowed corner. He wrapped his arms around her waist, lips grazing the back of her neck. Like the caress of a winter breeze.

"The realtor—"

"Is gone," he said in a quiet voice as he left a trail of kisses above her camisole. "It's just us, Princess."

Her head tipped back onto his shoulder as the pulsing between her legs intensified ever so slightly. "That's not what the chastity belt was for."

"It's not...*not* what it's for." His hand trailed up her chest and cupped her breast. "To remind you who you belong to."

"Gods, you're—" The words died on her lips as the vibration stopped. Her core ached. "Evil."

The only reply was his dark, amused hum. "The new place needs a proper welcome."

"You know I can just take it off?"

"Yeah…but you won't."

Heat pooled between her legs. The chastity belt had been a concession, one she had hesitated to make. What kind of modern woman wore something from the medieval times? But then Isidore had made a compelling argument for some of its perks. She would be traveling alone at times in the Andes as a woman with a magic aura that made people want to get a bit too close. The belt was magicked to protect her from sexual assault. Only the two of them could remove it, and there was something tantalizing about knowing he could tease her even from thousands of miles away. Dangerous too. He *could* activate it while she was working, but the relationship contract they'd worked out said he wouldn't. They had also agreed that she would only take it off if he could watch her, so he didn't miss an opportunity to absorb her energy.

She whimpered as he pushed her shirt up. His hand was cool on her stomach, teasing as he inched closer to the soft leather of the chastity belt. Magic held it in place on her hips, and it was more comfortable than any underwear she'd ever worn.

"I can feel your need, Princess. All it would take is one brush…" His fingertips were under the waist of her jeans. Inching closer and closer. Then he pulled away. "But first I have something for you."

Her breath was coming in short gasps, and she only just managed to turn around. "You fix this."

His lips were curved into his most charming grin. "Say please."

"Isidore…" A cooling sensation replaced the coiling heat, dousing the embers as the chastity belt did what it was *actually* designed for. To cool her down if she was aroused, so she saved her energy for him. She let out a relieved sigh. "Thank you."

"We're not done, but I do want to give you something first." His expression sobered, and he reached into his pocket. "I promised I'd replace the amulet, and a Crimson Fang always delivers." He extracted a black velvet jewelry box, then opened it.

She gaped at the gorgeous gold choker necklace. Magic danced along interweaving metal threads, and it came to a point just where it would sit at the hollow of her collarbone. A peridot pendant dangled in its center.

"It's got some…extras to it. Lamia demon stuff…It will mark you as mine."

Her gaze darted up to his face. "A collar?"

Isidore cleared his throat and shifted nervously. "Yeah, kind of. But usually the ones my cabal gives to our prey-partners can't be removed by anyone but the lamia that places it. You'll be able to take it off. You don't have to wear it…But it will mute your aura, without forcing your divine essence back into a closet. If you have an encounter with a human with magic sight or another chaos being it will make you look like a protective nishutu." She stared at the shimmering peridot stone. Her aura had become more potent since she'd fully transformed, and even casual encounters with humans had become a delicate dance. To mitigate the issue, she'd been staying home. Their house hunting had been done on Zillow, and then Isidore had video called her to view a place. This was the first time she'd left the townhouse in weeks. *And I'm getting on a plane in three days to go thousands of miles away.*

"You'll learn how to control it."

She snapped her head up to meet his determined emerald gaze. The tension left her body as she let out the breath she'd been holding. Of course she could control it. Gordon didn't wear his amulet all the time; the last time she saw him he'd been without it. If he could control his aura in a near-constant drunken stupor, surely she could figure it out. "Thanks. Germund?"

He licked his lips. "I don't think he'll bother you while you're away. With any luck he'll assume you died. International travel is a pain and finding you on a mountain somewhere will be difficult. More than likely he'll lick his wounds and bide his time. But if he does try something? I'll know, because I'll be watching his every move. If the worst happens, I'll be able to find you with the locator spell in the collar…On top that Breath of Life ability I discovered, where I can feel the general direction you're in."

The tone in his voice made it clear he was barely maintaining his facade of calm. But his expression gave him away as his gaze trailed her neck, and she knew he was already imagining the choker—the collar—secured in place. Marking her as his. Excitement sent her heart fluttering. It was better than her amulet. Her people had wanted to erase her. What Isidore offered was protection, a home. A promise that someone cared enough to make sure she didn't disappear in the night. She blinked rapidly, clearing the moisture gathering in her lashes. "I can take it off anytime I want?"

"Yes."

A month ago, she would have balked at the idea of wearing something like this. It should have felt like a shackle. But now? She felt safe and wanted. A slow, undeniable ember burned in her stomach. "I accept," she purred.

His mouth hung open for half a second. Then a shiver of excitement made his aura flicker. His eyes glimmered in that possessive, territorial way that told her she'd done something that made his demon happy. "Turn around."

A smile touched her lips as she put her back to him, and she lifted her ponytail so he could drape the collar around her neck. Magic sizzled as the clasp sealed shut. It weighed itself down, anchoring her in this moment. Anchoring her to him. She turned around and their noses almost brushed. "You'll really wait to feed until we're together?" That had been her demand. The thought of her lamia feeding on anyone else had her hackles rising.

He caressed her cheek. "There's no one on earth I want to touch but you. I'll visit you in July, like we planned. It will be hell waiting for you, but I'll be fine with the blood I can get from my dealer until then, as long as you let me..." He leaned forward, kissing along her jaw. His fangs lightly dragged down her neck.

A shiver ran through her. They would wait together,

even with miles between them. A quiet purr rumbled in her throat. "When?"

"Mm...so eager..." He pulled away and lifted her chin. "Tomorrow. I'll have a temporary arrangement set up by then. When you come back, I'll make sure we have an appropriate place for our feeding rituals. Somewhere secluded, away from the house. I need to keep it separate."

She leaned into him. "And your family?"

His eyes flared as he ran his fingers down her neck and rested his hand on her shoulder. "As far as I'm concerned, the only thing that matters is the relationship agreement we negotiated. I don't want to own you, we're equal partners..." His lips twitched into a mischievous smile. "Except during the feeding ritual. Then you're mine."

A flutter left her breathless as he looped his arm around her waist, securing her against his hip. Their eyes locked. Her heart skipped a beat and heat washed over her. He leaned closer, and their lips met. A perfect harmony of magic danced around them. Green and indigo mixed with gold and earthen colors. She knew the road ahead wouldn't be smooth, but it was one she wouldn't be traveling alone.

"In the meantime..." His voice dropped, velvety and dark against her ear. "Let me show you what it means to belong to a lamia prince."

THANK YOU FOR READING

Craving more chaotic tenderness and magical disaster romance?

Book Two of the Nocturne Cage Trilogy, *Dissonant Desires*, arrives September 2025—but you can get exclusive short stories (and secrets) delivered straight to your inbox by joining my newsletter!

Just scan the QR code or visit:
https://kitenglardauthor.substack.com

ACKNOWLEDGMENTS

First and foremost, I want to thank my editor, Shawna Hampton, for her tireless efforts in wrangling my literary gremlins into a final draft polished to a shine.

Deep thanks to my cover artist, Stewart Williams, for creating such gorgeous art, and for walking me through the many steps of publishing when I had no idea what I was doing.

A huge thank you to my husband, for letting me read every version of this book out loud to him, chapter by chapter.

Thank you to my incredible family, and especially to my in-laws, Bill and Carol Aronoff, for their continued support as I've stumbled my way into becoming a full-time writer.

I'm especially grateful to Charlotte McBride for reading every one of the worst drafts and helping me fine-tune this story into what it is now.

And finally, thank you to *National Geographic*. Without it, this book would not exist. It captured my imagination at a young age and got me hooked on ancient cultures, myth, and climate science.

ABOUT THE AUTHOR

KIT ENGLARD is a fantasy author whose work draws on Mesopotamian mythology, Critical Disability Theory, and her lived experience as a DeafBlind woman. As graduate of Chatham University, she grew up in Pittsburgh, and is overjoyed to have spent her time following her characters through the streets of her favorite city.

When not writing about demons, chaos magic, or mythical creatures hiding in plain sight, Kit can be found hiking with her guide dog, getting lost in obscure mythological texts, or speaking about disability representation in speculative fiction.